Last Warning

Everyone told Blair that her landlady, Ann Kenyon, was eccentric to say the least. Some even called her insane, a woman obsessed by the idea that all men were evil and murderous by nature.

So Blair felt quite safe in ignoring Ann's warnings about Glen Forbes. Her hints that such an appealing, ideal man meant danger and death for any woman unfortunate enough to get involved with him seemed foolish.

But now Blair could no longer ignore these warnings—just as Ann could no longer offer them. For Ann Kenyon lay murdered in bed, and as Blair stared down at the grotesque corpse, she desperately wondered who was the mad one . . .

. . . Ann, in her lonely spinster's world of suspicion and hysterical fear . . . ?

. . . or herself, in a fool's paradise of love that was swiftly turning into a hellish nightmare?

The Last Gamble

Rae Foley

A DELL BOOK

For the Babes in the Woods
Eleanor and Hugh Hopkins

Published by
DELL PUBLISHING CO., INC.
1 Dag Hammarskjold Plaza
New York, New York 10017

The characters, places, incidents and situations
in this book are imaginary and have no relation
to any person, place or actual happening

1

"If they'd just come out and accuse me of murder I could deal with it—in one way or another. What is breaking me down is this silent treatment."

For some time Blair Masters had been aware of the murmur of voices from the next room. Now one of them rose in the most arresting statement she had ever heard a man make. In belated caution the voice dropped again.

If that was the voice of the man she had come to see, Blair decided, she had better get out of the house without delay. But what perfectly foul luck it would be to lose a chance like this. From the moment she had seen the house she had fallen in love with the warm red brick, the delicate iron grillwork, the beautiful white doorway. Whoever had set it perfectly on Gramercy Park had loved it.

Even the ponderous furniture could not spoil its gracious lines. Already she had mentally tossed out ugly cabinets and cumbersome tables, replacing them with pieces she remembered seeing in Madison Avenue shops. She was busy flooding the drawing room with light and color, giving it back the grace that was its heritage. Her creative instinct had caught fire. Until she had transformed the house she could not bear to leave it.

But—murder? Surely Dr. Evans would not have sent her to someone who was involved in murder. After all, he was Mr. Potter's physician; he had known the man all his life. What had he said, anyhow?

"It will be good for you to work for Hiram Potter

and you will be good for him. You can turn that mausoleum of his into a place a man can live in, make it bright and cheerful. God knows he could use a little cheerfulness."

"What's wrong with the man?" Blair had asked.

"He has had rather a beastly time. The girl he loved was locked up a few months ago for the rest of her life as criminally insane."

Blair had shivered and then had given the elderly doctor a suspicious look. He grinned at her. "After all," he pointed out, "you're getting on, you know. Twenty-six. Gather your rosebuds while you may."

"Are you trying to provide me with a client or with a husband?" she asked coldly.

"Speaking as a friend," he had replied, unperturbed by her smoldering indignation, "it strikes me that you need both. And no back talk, young lady. You are too attractive to be unattached. How long have you been buried in a small town, looking after a sick old woman? And what have you done with your energy and all your dreams? Worked to prepare yourself for a career. Career," he snorted. "You haven't begun to live. The purpose of living, after all, is to live. Why don't people discover that? Too simple for them, of course. The young never take anything seriously if it sounds simple."

When Blair laughed he said, "Laugh if you like. Just the same, go on as you are doing for another five years, too busy to waste time falling in love, and you know what will happen."

"I know," Blair told him wearily. "A spinster. An old maid. A soulless career woman. I heard that from my aunt at least once a week."

"Not at all," the doctor retorted. "You'll fall in love, of course. Bound to. But did you ever stop to think of the men over whom intelligent women lose their heads? You're apt to fall for someone whom your more experienced friends would sheer off from at sight, some professional lady killer."

Blair had laughed outright and it was a pleasant

sound. "So far no movie actor has stirred my pulse."

There was amusement as well as irony in his face. "Rather a pity. You don't know what you've missed. Though the really dangerous men, where women are concerned, tend to be ordinary enough in appearance. Casanova was no beauty. And the real, the actual lady killers, were downright homely. Bluebeard wasn't handsome, so far as I ever heard, but he must have had a potent attraction for women."

With the freedom of an old friend Dr. Evans had turned her so that she faced a long mirror and she looked at the reflection of the tall girl in the beautifully cut gray suit with a crisp white blouse, a small gray hat on hair that was nearly black. She had long eyes of smoky blue with thick lashes and eyebrows that tilted at her temples. They were, as she was well aware, her one good feature. Her nose was just a nose and her mouth was too large.

"You are no beauty," her aunt had once told her frankly, "but there is something about you that makes people turn for a second look. You've got an interesting face and, if you'd only use it, a lot more charm than anyone needs."

Beside her stood Dr. Evans, square and ruddy, smiling at her. In spite of her annoyance, Blair found herself smiling back.

"I don't need a husband," she had told him then, "but I do need a job. I'll do my best to make Mr. Potter's house lovely for him and if the job pays well I'll have a start toward a decorating shop of my own somewhere."

What she refrained from telling him was how desperately she needed the job. Her bank account held exactly fifty-four dollars, which would not cover another month's rent on her one-room apartment, let alone provide her with food. The long illness and death of the aunt who had educated her had wiped out her small capital, except for train fare to New York, one good suit and a month's living. If the Potter job fell through she would have to clerk in a store until something more promising developed.

But—murder? Who would speak of murder in this tranquil Gramercy Park house?

A quiet voice said, "Miss Masters? I'm so sorry you've been kept waiting. I am Hiram Potter."

He was a fair, elegant young man with hair as sleek as though it had been polished; a pleasant but unrevealing face and an unstressed voice which could never be mistaken for the vibrant one that had just electrified her.

Too well trained to be human, was her unspoken comment as she found herself settled in a more comfortable chair, a small table unobtrusively rolled beside her with an ashtray, cigarette box and lighter, and her host was mixing highballs at a shiny bar, which was obviously a new acquisition and clashed with the Victorian furniture. Her eyes widened as she saw the size of his own drink which he disposed of in a few hasty swallows. He poured a second drink for himself, brought one to her and pulled up a chair to face her.

"I needed that." He set down his glass and stared at it, frowning.

Blair, aware that his attention was on something or someone else, sipped her drink and waited. She was amused to see the start with which he abruptly noticed her.

"Sorry," he said. "I guess I'm a little muddled." He pushed the ashtray closer to her and mentioned their mutual friend, Dr. Evans. "A delightful old fellow but he will persist in laboring under the delusion that patients want commonsense instead of magic. Not," he hastened to add, "that I blame them for that. I'm all on the side of magic myself. Within reason, of course."

"It all depends, I suppose, on what you think is reasonable."

"Anything within the bounds of sanity," he said, and seemed surprised at his own words. Once more the frown cut deeply into his forehead and again she felt that he had forgotten her, that he was grappling with some problem of his own.

There was nothing awkward about the silence. Blair leaned back in her chair relaxed. There was one nice thing about Mr. Potter. He was no trouble to talk to. It was a relief not to feel that she had to be crisp and incisive and sell him brightly on the idea that she was the only possible decorator for him. She looked up to encounter a bright, interested gaze. Confound the man! He was more astute than he appeared, deliberately encouraging her to relax, to let down her guard. Had she looked too eager, too tense, betrayed how much the job meant to her?

"How's your drink?"

"Fine. No, not another."

"Not so tired now?"

As she looked her question he waved at the ugly furniture. "Moving all this stuff out. Tiresome work."

Even while she laughed Blair flushed at the accuracy with which he read her thoughts. He had no right to be so at home in her mind.

"Awful, isn't it?" he said cheerfully. "There have been times when I thought the simplest and most satisfying way to deal with it would be to set fire to the whole lot."

It was the undercurrent of savagery in his tone that surprised her. "We won't have to do anything as drastic as that," she said lightly. "The house itself is so lovely that—"

"Since I talked to Dr. Evans," he said, "I've been wondering whether it wouldn't be best to let the place go till autumn. My plans have changed and I'll be spending the summer in Connecticut."

Blair's sick disappointment was so great that she had to make an effort to hold the pleasant, noncommittal smile on her lips. The cigarette snapped in her fingers and she bent her dark head over the ashtray while she crushed it out. Smile, she ordered herself, and managed to raise her head.

"What I had in mind," Mr. Potter went on smoothly, as though he had not observed her ebbing color, her shocked eyes, her determined smile, "was that you might postpone this job until, oh, say October, and take on something different for the next six months."

"I'm not trained for anything but decorating," she said bluntly, and in her mind heard her aunt's despairing wail, "Use a little charm, Blair, for heaven's sake."

"Do you know anything about American antiques?"

"Oh, yes, that's part of the job, of course. Well," her incurable honesty rose up to confront her, "I know periods. But if you mean a real expert—"

"But at least you know the patter. I always assumed that the patter was practically the first thing a decorator learns. Then he spends the rest of his life figuring out what it means. Like that peculiar vocabulary the art critics use. Obscure but impressive."

Blair grinned at him. "Would you pluck out the heart of my mystery?"

"My crystal ball is in the repair shop," Mr. Potter admitted. "Without it I am helpless. But at a guess you are in your middle twenties, probably an only child; you've been submerged chiefly by your own fault because you are one of those self-sacrificing females who has lived someone else's life up to now. You are from an ugly community or an environment that could not satisfy your love for beauty. You have a lot of intelligence though not as much as you believe; a great deal more, ah, attractiveness than you suspect; and," to her surprise he looked troubled, "you are a bit gullible, I think."

"Well," Blair expelled a long breath, "I'd hate to see what you can do when that crystal ball is functioning. What was wrong with it?"

"It reflected what I was looking for instead of what was there." For a shaken moment Blair saw beneath the lightness of manner into somber depths and then Mr. Potter shut her out. "Did I hit it?"

"Right on the nail. What is that six-months job?"

He hesitated. "On second thought, the idea probably isn't so good."

"Why? Because you think I am gullible? For some reason that seems to bother you."

"This isn't fair," he protested. "You are supposed to leave the mind-reading to me. I don't think the job would suit you."

There was a finality in his tone that made clear he had decided not to offer her the job. In one lavish gesture Blair tossed away all the lessons she had learned on Making a Good Impression and Building Up Your Own Importance. Any job, she said, would be a godsend. Whether she liked it or not was irrelevant. Whether it offered a future or not was unimportant. Eventually she planned to have her own shop and she was pretty sure she was equipped to make a success of it, but temporarily she had to have an income of some sort. If not the job he had in mind then clerking in a store or waiting on tables at Child's.

As usual when she had been guilty of an outburst she longed to take back her words. What would this beautifully dressed, bland young man know about needing a job? A perfectly trained robot, that's what he was. Because she was angry with herself she turned her anger on him.

He picked up his glass and drank, studying her over it. Blair found herself revising her ideas. Perhaps this man would not be so easy to deal with.

"Do you like to gamble?" he asked abruptly.

She was taken aback. "I don't know. I've never really done any gambling."

He drained his glass and set it down with the air of a man who has come to a decision. "You'd really like a shot at this job?" When she nodded he said, "All right. I'll tell you about it. Have you heard of Bridgetown?"

She shook her head.

Bridgetown, he explained, was one of those story-book Connecticut villages with a winding river, big elms, red maples, a covered bridge, a white church with a high steeple. At least, that's what it had been. A reasonably well-to-do community with no spectacular wealth and no real want. Then the factories in a near-by industrial town, which had provided most of the employment, began to move south, lured by a promise of escaping taxes. Unemployment was spreading, there was some real suffering, there probably would be more. People lamented and talked and shook their heads and said there ought to be a law but nobody did anything. Then two rival solutions came up.

Progress, improvement and efficiency had raised their ugly heads. One of the town fathers had come into rather a lot of money—Mr. Potter broke off for a moment as though listening to his own words in surprise.

"He'd like to make it breed and multiply," he went on. "There is a big tract of land on the edge of the village that he planned to buy up for a real estate development: neat lines of prefabricated summer cottages complete with television aerials and all the trees cut down to make ten feet of lawn."

"Oh, dear!"

"A friend of mine declared, more or less, 'Over my dead body,' and bought the land. He started designing the Bridgetown Center. I don't know much about it except that he is trying to maintain the original character of the village and provide outlets for handcrafts of all sorts. Enable people to support themselves and still keep their roots in the land so they won't have to become migratory labor. As it happens, he needs an assistant to run an antique shop that is part of the project."

Blair felt the color burning in her face. "I'm sorry, Mr. Potter. I didn't mean to give the impression that I felt you owed me a job simply because you aren't ready to do over your house. It is kind of you but, after all, I have sense enough to realize you can't walk a mile in New England without falling over someone who knows antiques."

"Actually," he said, "it happens to be true. Glen Forbes can't get local help. The only worry I have is not about recommending you for the job but about recommending the job to you. Of course, I'll be in Bridgetown myself, although—"

As the job began to fade from her grasp, in the face

of Mr. Potter's inexplicable reluctance, Blair grew determined not to lose it. Selling antiques in a small town was not like decorating a New York townhouse. It was, however, better than selling hats to middle aged women who always expected a new hat to rejuvenate them, bringing them nearer to the heart's desire, and blamed the clerk when it didn't.

"What salary is he offering?"

"A hundred and a quarter a week."

"A hun—" Blair sat bolt upright. "What's wrong with that job?"

"I'm not sure," Mr. Potter said in a tone of misgiving. "That's the real problem, you see. I'm not sure."

2

Since the day of the interview on Gramercy Park Blair
Masters had not seen Mr. Potter, though he had called
her twice on the telephone. The first time he had told
her that Glen Forbes was delighted to learn that she
would take the job and that he would expect her in ten
days. On the second occasion he explained that he had
been inquiring about a place where she could live and
thought he had found something that would do.

"Good heavens," Blair expostulated, "there is no
reason why you should do all this."

"Well, there is, in a way. I'm responsible for you.
And Bridgetown doesn't have the usual accommodations for summer people. But there is a woman who is
willing to give you room and board. There's no choice
actually. It seems to be Miss Kenyon or else."

Blair groaned to herself. After being supervised all
her life by her aunt she was going to be supervised for
the summer by a small-town spinster.

"She's not doing this just as a favor to you, is she?"

"Not at all. I've never met the woman. How suspicious you are," he added mildly, "although it's a useful
trait in the circumstances. Not endearing, perhaps, but
I'm delighted you have it." He went on so quickly that
Blair had no opportunity to summon up words that
would be sufficiently blighting. "Miss Kenyon is eager
to have a paying guest. She's rather hard up, I believe.
She writes and doesn't quite make a living at it. You
may have heard of her. Ann Kenyon."

"It's the kind of name I feel I ought to remember
but I can't place it."

"I'll be driving up day after tomorrow. If you are ready by then, I'd like to take you along. Ten o'clock all right?"

Blair thanked him. "I suppose," she said, thinking aloud, "if I'm going to be in the country for six months I'll have to do something about a car of my own."

"I wouldn't advise that. No, I really wouldn't advise that, Miss Masters."

On the whole, she thought savagely, as she locked the last suitcase, she'd have been wiser to take a job in a store. Of course, it wouldn't have paid a hundred and twenty-five dollars a week but if things went on as they had started she would earn every penny. An employer so disagreeable the local people wouldn't work for him; Mr. Potter constituting himself her guardian, deciding where she would live and whether she should buy a car; and a small-town spinster to watch every move she made. Ann Kenyon. The name was vaguely familiar and for some reason it carried an unpleasant association.

Beggars, she reminded herself, can't be choosers. Which was a silly thing to think. Demoralizing. She wasn't a beggar and she'd try hard to do her job satisfactorily. If not for her own sake, then for Mr. Potter's. After all, she had really driven him into a corner. He had not wanted her to take the job. Something about it seemed to bother him.

When she had put on a dress of rose wool she had knitted herself she bent closer to the mirror to apply a matching lipstick and study her reflection. The dress fitted perfectly and was more becoming than she had anticipated.

"You don't look like a beggar," she told herself in approval. "Stop worrying. You're young and it's spring and anything could happen." She thought about Dr. Evans and laughed softly. "And high time," she added, "that something does happen."

Promptly at ten o'clock Mr. Potter tapped at her door, gathered up her suitcases and stacked them neatly in the trunk of a yellow convertible whose spectacular lines took Blair's breath away.

"Silly, isn't it?" he commented as he helped her into the front seat. "That's reaction for you. After striving to be the invisible man for the first twenty-eight years of my life, I discovered that I didn't really give a damn whether people looked at me or not. If it amuses them, let them look. At least, the thing runs."

He threaded his way through traffic, his attention engrossed by plunging trucks and erratic taxis. When a pedestrian ran in front of the car he stopped with a screaming of brakes.

"If you're so hell bent on suicide," he snarled, "why can't you do it at home? You'll make a repulsive corpse."

Blair found herself laughing but her companion continued to scowl. As he took the ramp onto the West Side Highway he said, "Sorry if I seem to be in a filthy humor this morning."

On the parkways farther north forsythia had already given way to pink and white dogwood and the tips of maples made a faint red glow against the sky. Blair took a quick glance at him while he was preoccupied by traffic. What on earth was she getting herself into? She was committed for six months to work with a man she had never seen, introduced by a man whom she barely knew. An unpredictable man about whom she had already thrown out her first impressions. And she was leaving behind her New York City which had been her goal for the past five years. As they went farther north traffic dwindled increasingly and she had an impulse to say, "Let me out! I'm going back."

"Actually," Mr. Potter said, plunging into her mind with uncanny accuracy, "it won't be so bad. Bridgetown is a pleasant spot and, if you catch any of Forbes' enthusiasm, you'll find the job interesting. He will give you a free hand. That's really the bond between us; not that we belong to the same fraternity but that he's one of the last individualists out of captivity."

Again he seemed to listen to himself in surprise. "It's curious, isn't it, that such statements can become literally true? As for Miss Kenyon—"

"Bluebeard!" Blair exclaimed. "I knew the woman's name was familiar. It ought to be. She does psychological true-life stories about men who were mass murderers. My aunt loved them and I read them aloud to her. They were horrible. The author was—I don't know how to describe the impression she made on me. Ghoulish. Gloating. Her hatred of men was pathological."

Mr. Potter was silent while he passed a car and returned to the right-hand lane. Then he said, "Good God! I had no idea of that."

"It doesn't matter," Blair assured him. "Unless, of course, she expects to talk about her work. I don't believe I could take much of that. I don't like people who seem to—hover over cruelty. In a way, cruelty is the only thing that strikes me as completely unforgivable. The unpardonable sin."

"But I understood—you see, she was recommended by an old friend of my mother's, a Mrs. Brenning whom I'm going to visit. All she said was that the woman was a writer who would take in a paying guest to eke out her income."

His disturbance struck Blair as incommensurate with the situation. Obviously her landlady was going to be tiresome but there was no occasion for Mr. Potter's anxiety. And yet, recalling the Kenyon books, Blair was conscious of more than mere distaste.

Her companion withdrew fathoms deep into his thoughts and did not emerge until they stopped at an inn. Over an excellent lunch he pulled out a notebook.

Blair, who was watching in enchantment while three white swans floated on a miniature pond under weeping willows, turned in surprise when he asked, "Do you remember the titles of those Kenyon books?"

"You'd hate them!" she protested.

"I expect so. Still, I had better read them."

Any man who took the trouble to read a writer's books before meeting her ought to be preserved in a museum, she thought. Aloud she said, "The one on

Landru was called *Why Did He Kill Them?,* the George Joseph Smith was *Watery Graves.* There were others: Dr. Crippen, I think, and Dr. Pritchard. Men who were—monstrous. At least, that was the impression she gave. A kind of murky horror, a vicious—" she made a helpless gesture. "They were beastly books about beastly people. Why on earth you want to read them unless mass murder is a hobby of yours—"

He was silent and Blair, remembering the news stories which, at Dr. Evans' suggestion, she had looked up at the library, was appalled at what she had done. That girl Mr. Potter had loved—how many people had she killed?—three or four, at least.

For the first time she wondered why the news stories had made so little impression on her. She supposed the reason was that she had met Mr. Potter beforehand and she simply could not assimilate the fact that so retiring and unassuming a man had played so violent a part in a series of murders; that, after seeing him, she could not visualize him tracking down a killer, particularly in the company of a comely young model. Like many other people she began to wonder, a little uneasily, whether there might not be more to the young man than she had assumed.

"A hobby," he repeated at last, his voice colorless, "no, not that. But when one sees the havoc, the tragedy that can be caused by instability—do you know Aristotle?"

Blair realized with gratitude that he had shifted the whole discussion into the realm of the impersonal. *"The Poetics,* but not since I left school."

"Aristotle believed in the 'fatal flaw' in human character, the flaw that inevitably produces tragedy. It seems to me that if one could detect the flaw before the damage is done one might prevent the catastrophe. But, of course—look here, Miss Masters, would you like to go back? I'll explain to Forbes."

Aware that the eleven dollars remaining in her handbag now represented her all, Blair smiled rather grimly. Her chief anxiety was that her landlady would require a week's rent in advance.

"Miss Kenyon doesn't sound that bad," she said.

Mr. Potter gave her a troubled look. "It's just possible that I've made rather a bad mistake. Sometimes I think that though I don't do much myself I seem to—make things happen."

"A kind of catalytic agent," she suggested.

"Something like that. But I don't want anything to happen to you."

Blair smiled in amusement. "You know, I was thinking this morning that it's about time something happened to me."

Mr. Potter did not return the smile. He paid the bill and drew her chair back as she got up. "We'll be there in another hour. Too bad it's so early in the season. You'll find the landscape rather bleak until the leaves come out."

As he drove just a hair's breadth within the bounds of safety Blair had little awareness of the landscape beyond great stark trees, a narrow winding road with a cliff on one side and a river on the other, and in the distance blue hills. It occurred to her that he had deliberately set a pace which made conversation impracticable.

At length he slowed to a crawl, made a sharp right turn and eased the long car through a covered bridge, clattering over loose floor boards. On the other side, the main road turned to the left between bare elms that later would arch over it. A narrow road, lined by a slim row of white birches, branched to the right.

"And this," he said briskly, "is the Bridgetown Center. Suppose I leave you here and take your luggage to Miss Kenyon's. I'll pick you up in a couple of hours and see that you get settled."

"I'm being a frightful nuisance," Blair lamented as she got out of the car.

"Not at all. And remember, Miss Masters, you aren't committed in the least. If you aren't quite happy here you can leave on the first train."

Blair nodded, waved her hand and turned toward

the Bridgetown Center. Only a beginning had been made but it was on a scale she had not anticipated. A village green had been laid out, trees planted, a lawn with flower beds. On one side there was a perfect salt box. Next to it the replica of a town hall, as yet unfinished. Set back from the green was a red barn where painters were adding white trim to doors and windows. A bulldozer was digging an excavation for another building.

It was so charming that she stood smiling to herself in sheer pleasure. All at once her spirits soared. What on earth had she been worrying about? Everything was going to be wonderful. Simply wonderful.

An unobtrusive plaque on the salt box read: *Office*. Blair opened the door and walked into a wide hallway with a circular staircase in the rear, rag rugs on polished oak boards, and daffodils in a blue vase. The place smelled of fresh paint. On either side there were closed doors.

She was about to call out, announcing her presence, when she heard a vibrant voice that stopped her in her tracks, an unmistakable voice, the one that had spoken to Mr. Potter about murder, back in Gramercy Park.

"I've given you every chance," it said, "But I'm neither a fool nor an easy mark. You've been juggling the books consistently. They're a mess. So far as I can tell, you are about three thousand dollars short. What in hell have you done with the money, George? Played the market? Races? Got a girl somewhere?"

"It's not as though you would miss it," was the sullen reply.

"You mean," the other man said incredulously, "that I'm supposed to let it go, just write it off? Is that the way you want it?"

There was no answer.

"And why am I to play Santa Claus? I gave you the job because you are Evelyn's cousin. But I'm damned if I'll sit back and watch you line your pockets at my expense."

"If I were you, Glen," said the second man, "I wouldn't make any threats."

A chair scraped back, there were quick footsteps, the door on the left opened and a young man came out hurriedly, banging the door behind him. He stopped short when he saw Blair. What struck her most were the tiny features in a large face, small eyes, small mouth, a button of a nose. He straightened his tie.

"I didn't hear you come in. We haven't opened for business yet."

"I am Blair Masters." When he merely smiled and waited, she went on, "I—that is, Mr. Forbes has engaged me to run the antique shop for the season."

He was stupid with surprise. Then something flickered in the small eyes. He surveyed her from head to foot with a touch of insolence. "That's news. Big news."

I can't afford to lose my temper, Blair reminded herself. She said frigidly, "Will you please tell Mr. Forbes I am here?"

"This is going to be a pleasure." He opened the door. "Oh, Glen," he drawled, "your new—that is, Miss Masters has arrived."

"Fine! Bring her in, will you?"

There was a large desk in the room, a couple of maple chairs, logs crackling cheerfully in the fireplace and above them on the mantel a large water-color sketch. What arrested Blair's attention, however, was the man who rose from behind the desk to greet her. A man of medium height with thick shoulders, heavy crisp brown hair, a brown face with the skin pulled taut over good bones, gray eyes that were curiously light in the dark face. She was aware that George was watching them both with avid curiosity.

"Miss Masters?" The voice, vibrant and deep, was, beyond all doubt, the voice she had heard at Mr. Potter's house. "I am Glen Forbes. It was good of you to come." The hand that grasped hers was warm and muscular. She had an uncomfortable impression of unleashed force, of smoldering vitality. "Sit down, won't you? Oh, this is George Harrison, our accountant. Miss Masters is going to be my assistant this season, George. We're very lucky to get her."

"I'll say we are." There was a hint of a snicker in George's voice and then, to Blair's relief, he withdrew across the hall and ostentatiously closed his door.

Blair settled herself in the maple rocker and looked up to find Glen Forbes studying her intently. Instead of returning to his chair he came around to lean on the desk so that he could face her. She had a curious illusion that he was towering over her, too close, and fought down an impulse to push back her chair.

I've worked with too many women, she thought in a panic. I'll never be able to cope with this man. Never in the world.

"How much did Potter tell you?" he asked abruptly.

"Just that you needed someone for the season."

He searched her face as though looking for something he failed to find. "I thought," he said in a tone of dissatisfaction, "that you'd be older. However—I hope you won't find it too difficult. You'll be pretty much on your own. I can handle most of the project but I'm out of my depth in antiques."

"You mean I'm the only assistant you have?" she asked in surprise.

His face darkened. "Temporarily, at least. I hope in time—of course, I could get more people from New York but, after all, the idea was to make it a local project."

The fact that local people would not work for him was so embarrassingly obvious that he abandoned any attempt at explanation. With a quick movement he went toward the fireplace.

"I have only begun, of course. This is what I hope it will be like in time."

Blair stood beside him looking at the sketch of the projected Center. The buildings she had seen were only a small part of the plan. The whole thing was charmingly designed and there was wit as well as skill in the tiny figures that peopled the sketch, moving across the miniature green, entering the buildings that surrounded it, their microscopic faces like faintly malicious portraits.

A nervous brown hand pointed from building to building: a small gallery for displaying local art, a shop for the sale of hooked rugs and other handcrafts, a little theater.

"No rival to Tanglewood, of course, or even to Stratford," Forbes said, "but an opportunity for young artists to get a hearing without all the financial gamble of a Town Hall debut."

"It's a terrific idea," Blair said enthusiastically, "but is there room for all this?" ·

"There is plenty of land. I own it and I've left things so that the community will have enough money to maintain it. For some years, at any rate. Naturally, I hope that eventually it will not only become self-supporting but that it will bring outside money into Bridgetown."

"How grateful the people must be to you!"

Again the curiously light eyes raked her face, looking for something they failed to find. "Gratitude is too much to expect," he said dryly. "But when they find a really workable solution to some of their financial problems—there is growing poverty around here, Miss Masters, and I am convinced that we could—well, I won't bore you with all this today, though I warn you, I may ask your help now and then outside your own department."

Unexpectedly he smiled, a delightful smile. Why, she thought, startled, the man is immensely attractive.

"If you stay," he added.

"I can't imagine anything that would drive me away."

"Can't you?" he said oddly.

3

Outside the little white salt box a car came to a halt with a scream of brakes. Blair started at the sound and Forbes said gratingly, "God! Why can't that idiot learn to drive? They ought to take away his license."

A door banged and a moment later a man's shadow fell across the sill. As he entered the office Blair saw that he was startlingly like Glen Forbes in build and coloring; even their features were similar, although the newcomer's eyes were darker, his chin less aggressive. A younger brother, perhaps.

"Hi, Glen. I thought I'd find you here." He saw Blair and his eyes widened in pleased surprise. He had a gift, she thought, for making a woman feel lovely and desirable. Or it might just be practice.

"What the devil do you mean, Charlie, by driving like that?" Forbes snapped. "If I've told you once—" His anger seemed to be disproportionate to the offense. He spoke to the younger man as though he were an irresponsible teen-ager. Blair expected a furious retort but Charlie simply made a half-laughing gesture of exculpation.

"I was so blazing mad I clean forgot I was driving. Matter of fact, I've been fighting your battles for you, Glen."

"Thanks, I can fight my own."

Charlie, his eyes approving of Blair, lounged against the door frame. Compared with the older man's bottled-up energy, he seemed to be completely relaxed. "If you don't mind my saying so, you aren't making much headway. Not with Paul Brooks, anyhow."

"Keep out of this, Charlie!"

Blair moved away as unobtrusively as possible, trying to look as though absorption in the sketch of the Center had deafened her. If Charlie weren't blocking the doorway, she would have slipped outside to escape this family altercation. Curious that two men could be so alike and so dissimilar, one gay, the other somber; one indolent, the other dynamic; one engaging, the other—disturbing.

"Then you had better do something about it yourself," Charlie said with a touch of irritation. "I ran across Brooks at the *Gazette* when I was coming back from the bank—by the way, thanks for that deposit you made in my account—and he was trying to get them to run an editorial about the Center. Laying down the law in that pontifical manner of his. He said it wasn't just a case of standing in the way of progress and prosperity for our fair community. You know how he talks. He said this whole set-up stinks, that it's nothing more than a bribe to the village—" He broke off. Forbes had not moved but even Blair had a sense of danger from his terrible repression.

"So it's Brooks," he said tightly. "It has been Brooks all the time. But why, in God's name? Just to queer the Center?"

He was sunk in thought. At length he said, "The *Gazette* won't do it. I'd slap a libel suit on them and they know it." He jammed his hands in his pockets and stood with his shoulders hunched, a powerful compact body in which energy had been harnessed like caged steam, and shaken now by a fury that was almost, but not quite, out of control.

Charlie, Blair thought, knew more about women than he did about men. He did not seem to be aware of the fire he was fanning.

He nodded in agreement. "Yeah, that's what they told Brooks. So now he is going to call a town meeting and bring the thing out in the open. He's working on the people already. The small shopkeepers and services like the laundry would welcome a housing development and they don't know what to make of the Center."

Forbes barely stirred and yet Blair had a curious illusion that he rocked with a blow. For a moment she felt his disillusionment, his hurt, as sharply as though it were her own and anger flared in her against the unknown Brooks.

"Is that the way Bridgetown people really feel?" Forbes asked tonelessly. "They don't want the Center?"

Even Charlie was belatedly aware of the wound he had dealt. He said uneasily, "All I know is what Brooks said. I told the—" he looked at Blair and swallowed a word. "I said he ought to be satisfied with the three hundred thousand Connie left him.

"Drop it!" A vein throbbed in Forbes' temple. He scraped up the telephone from the desk and dialed a number. "Mr. Brenning, please . . . Glen Forbes . . . Stan? I want you to destroy my will. I'll call you in a few days about drawing another . . . yes, Charlie has just been telling me. You might have given me a hint . . . Even if Brooks doesn't represent the best interests of the community . . . No, I want it destroyed at once. Today. What does it matter whether I'm intestate for a week or so? . . . All right, I'll see you."

He set down the telephone, turned and remembered Blair. He introduced the other man as his cousin, Charles Forbes, and explained Blair's presence.

Like his cousin, Charlie had an engaging smile. "That's swell! You'll be a break for Glen and," he grinned, "one for me, I hope. It won't do to have you getting bored."

"You are probably boring her now," Forbes said shortly.

Outside, a woman's high clear voice said, "Oh, Charlie's here. Heavens, he's got another dent in the fenders. He shouldn't be at large." She followed her voice into the office accompanied by a stout, baldheaded, beaming man. "Oh, there you are, Charlie. I was just saying—"

He grinned at her. "We heard you, Emily."

"I suppose so," she said in resignation. "My voice does carry so but I can't seem to help it. Glen, dear!" She kissed him with warm affection. She bore a strong family resemblance to the two men; the same square, sturdy build; the same thick crisp hair, though hers had a few strands of white in it; the same brown face but warmer, softer. The features that made good-looking men made a plain woman. But she emanated a warmth, a vitality that would, Blair realized, always make her more attractive than prettier women.

The stout man said, "Emily and I were just passing."

Charlie laughed. "You and Emily heard that Paul Brooks had been sounding off and you came rushing in like the Marines to protect Glen."

The woman flushed. "Paul Brooks," she began furiously, "is a vindictive, unscrupulous—"

"Emily," the stout man said gently.

She looked at him, checked herself, smiled. "All right, Jerome, but just the same—"

Blair edged toward the window; in fact, she would have been glad to crawl through it, acutely embarrassed by the fact that she was continually impinging on personal problems that did not concern her. Forbes had appeared to forget her presence but he said, "Emily, this is Miss Masters who has promised to help me out this summer. My sister, Mrs. Cook. And Mr. Cook."

Emily took Blair's hand in both her own. "I'm so glad," she said with genuine pleasure. "Glen simply can't cope all by himself. I do hope you'll like it here. Jerome, isn't she charming?"

The stout man twinkled at her. "And if that embarrasses you, Miss Masters, imagine what it would be if Emily didn't like you. She'd be just as appallingly frank."

"I don't know how it is," Emily admitted, "but somehow things just pop out. I never realize what really dreadful things I think until I hear myself booming away. And a voice like a calliope, too. Socially, I am simply a disaster."

"Let's look at the bright side," Charlie consoled her. "You might have married a diplomat."

"God forbid" Emily said fervently. "International relations could never have stood the strain. It keeps Jerome busy patching up the terrific situations I create." She turned to Blair again. "But where are you to stay, my dear? Glen may not have thought of that. There are really no suitable—Jerome, if you'll move that old desk of yours out of the guest room, we could—"

Blair hastened to assure her that accommodations had been arranged at Miss Kenyon's.

"Kenyon? I don't know her."

"She's that broad-beamed female who wears the tight-fitting slacks," Charlie interposed. "I ran across her on the street the other day and picked up a package she had dropped. From the way she snatched it out of my hand you'd have thought I was trying to pick her up."

"She probably knows your reputation," Emily said. Her words fell into a sudden pool of silence. "Oh, dear! I didn't mean—in any case, Miss Masters, if you aren't comfortable don't hesitate to let me know. If Jerome will just move that desk—and I do want you to be happy. Glen really needs you so." Her husband touched her arm and she switched again.

"I wish I could ask you to dinner tonight, just to start you off right, but the Brennings are having a dinner party for their house guest and we've simply got to go." Again her patient husband touched her arm and she broke off with a little gasp of dismay. "Oh, Joan, I didn't see you. And really Jerome and I have been looking forward to the party. It was only because Miss Masters is a stranger here and—"

"Stop sputtering, Emily," Charlie advised her. "Hi, Joan."

"Hello, Charlie. Don't worry, Emily; we know you." The girl was small and blond and would have been extremely pretty if her features had been a degree less sharp. There was sharpness in her bones, sharpness in

her voice, sharpness in her eyes. She nodded carelessly
to Jerome Cook and tucked her hand possessively under Forbes' elbow. "How are you, darling? Mother is
outside." As she steered him to the door her eyes rested for a moment on Blair who felt like something at a
checking booth in a supermarket. The eyes rapidly tab-
ulated her dress, coat, shoes, the black hair which was
hatless.

"Joan's mother," Charlie warned Blair in a low tone
after the girl had disappeared with her captive, "comes
in only under escort like an ocean liner, but don't let
her floor you."

Before Blair could shape an answer, Forbes returned
with Joan and an older edition of herself in whom the
sharpening process had been accelerated by the years.
The latter nodded to the Cooks, ignored Charlie, and
then surveyed Blair, taking the introductions into her
own hands.

"You must be the young woman Mr. Potter mentioned to me. Miss Masters, I believe. I am Mrs. Stanley Brenning. I suggested a lodging for you. I hope it is
satisfactory."

Blair was careful to avoid Charlie's amused eyes
while she expressed the proper gratitude. She was
aware that Mrs. Brenning was summing her up and
found herself wondering whether the rose wool dress
fitted too well, whether she should have worn a hat.

"Mr. Potter, as you may know, is our house guest,
Miss Masters. At his suggestion I have asked your landlady, Miss Kenyon, to a small dinner party tonight, as
she is a writer and one must encourage the arts. I understand she is to prepare your meals so perhaps, in
that case," she looked dubiously at Blair, preparing for
a bold and dangerous move, "you had better come,
too."

Blair was thoroughly angry but before she could refuse Jerome Cook intervened. "Do come, Miss Masters. Otherwise Emily's evening will be ruined, worrying about you."

"And mine," Charlie put in.

Even Joan Brenning's laugh was sharp. "Don't be misled by Charlie," she advised Blair. "He makes a pass at every girl he sees."

Charlie winked at Blair. "Joan, you remind me more and more of a wren. Ever watch the females? They put a blade of grass in every possible nest just to establish squatter rights."

"Really, Charles," Mrs. Brenning expostulated, "I find that in execrable taste. Glen, I have my table planned. You won't back out at the last moment, will you?"

Forbes finished lighting a cigarette before he asked, "Why do you think I'll back out?"

"Well, Paul Brooks is coming. I had to ask him."

The light eyes narrowed as they watched her. "And you think Brooks will frighten me away?"

"You'll come then? Splendid." Mrs. Brenning looked around the office. "You've done a great deal with it already. But what is Miss Masters' work to be?"

"Miss Masters hasn't started work yet," Forbes said smoothly. "She is my guest today, and as it is nearly five o'clock, I suggest we adjourn to my rooms upstairs for cocktails."

"Not now. I have a thousand things to attend to. Come, Joan. Oh, Miss Masters, I told Mr. Potter we'd give you a lift, so if you are ready—"

"I'll run Miss Masters over to her place," Charlie suggested.

"No!" There was repressed violence in Forbes' voice. "I am responsible for Miss Masters. You aren't taking her anywhere, Charlie. Now or later."

Even then Blair knew that there was more than Charlie's careless driving behind Forbes' violence. The Cooks were motionless with shock. Joan's eyes flickered from face to face as though hoping to catch someone off guard. Mrs. Brenning was the only one to reveal approval.

"Oh, look here, Glen, really you—" Charlie met his cousin's eyes, color stained his face and faded out, leaving it gray.

"Miss Masters is coming with us," Emily Cook said quickly. "I want to see for myself that her room is adequate." She ignored Mrs. Brenning's outraged sniff. "We'll see you at seven."

Blair had a curious sensation of being hustled out of the shop between the Cooks.

"You're so slim we can all sit in front," Emily said as she led the way to an old Buick. Blair assumed that of the two other cars outside the house the Cadillac belonged to the Brennings and the Chevrolet to Charlie Forbes. The latter was a new model but the fenders were dented and one of the headlights was broken.

"Charlie really is a wretched driver but he's just careless. I'm sure Glen knows he is just careless. Accident prone. There are people like that. Accident prone." Emily repeated the phrase as though it comforted her. "Glen didn't mean—but he has changed so. So reserved. So suspicious. And I don't think that it's good for him to live alone here at the Center. Morbid."

"My dear," Jerome said in resignation, "they can probably hear every word you are saying."

His wife's troubled voice dwindled away. Jerome started the car, turned it. Emily exclaimed, "Where on earth are you going?"

The car clattered over loose floorboards in the covered bridge. When they had come out he said, "Miss Kenyon is renting the old Ramsay cottage down on the river bank."

"Oh, dear! But isn't there any other way to get to the place?"

The stout man's hand dropped from the wheel onto his wife's plump knee. "Just through the bridge and down the road in a hop, skip and jump. Miss Masters can walk to work in five minutes. Most convenient."

He turned off the highway onto a narrow dirt road that wound down to the river and a small brown cottage nestled among maples.

"Last stop," he said cheerfully.

When Blair had got out Emily said, "We'll see you tonight. In fact, we'll pick you up. Better wear evening dress. Mrs. Brenning expects it."

Jerome, making a difficult U-turn on the narrow road, did not speak. Apparently they had both forgotten about inspecting her room.

A screened porch ran across the front of the cottage with a view of the shallow river where boulders jutted up above the surface of the water. A woman came out wearing brown slacks that strained over her heavy hips and a shapeless gray jumper with a hole in one elbow. Her hair hung lankly around a face devoid of make-up. She was younger than Blair had expected, thirty-five at most, and somehow blurred as a person, as indistinct as though she were seen through water. Evidently she reserved for her work those savage touches of violence which Blair had detected in her books.

"You must be Miss Masters." She had the flat, ringless voice of the neurotic and the hand she submitted to be pressed was flaccid.

"It's nice of you to put me up, Miss Kenyon."

"Well," she said ungraciously, "you need the room and I need the money. What's nice about that?"

Ann Kenyon clumped across the porch and into an unexpectedly attractive living room with a vaulted ceiling, book-lined walls and furniture freshly covered with crisp chinz. "Kitchen's through there. Here's your bedroom, opening on the porch. The bath's between your room and mine. We'll have to share."

"This is fine," Blair said and meant it. The room was large, sunlit and airy, had a spool bed, a comfortable chair, a good light for reading and more closet space than she needed for her small wardrobe.

"Thirty-five a week with meals. But I'm not cooking tonight. We're both asked to a dinner party. Mrs. Stanley Brenning, the local social arbiter."

"I know. I just met Mrs. Brenning." Blair tossed her handbag on the chair and lifted the largest suitcase onto the luggage rack.

Miss Kenyon stood watching. "No one told me how long you expect to stay."

"Why—six months, I believe."

"That's fine. I've already spent the publisher's advance fixing up this place but I'll have my new book finished by then."

Blair lifted out dresses and laid them on the bed. Miss Kenyon watched stolidly.

"You'll find plenty of hangers in the closet and the dresser drawers are freshly lined."

"Thank you, I have everything I need," Blair said pointedly.

Miss Kenyon was not sensitive to tone. "I was wondering—six months in Bridgetown—"

Evidently she would not leave until her curiosity had been appeased. Blair explained that she planned to work in Bridgetown.

"Are you a writer, too?" Miss Kenyon successfully concealed any rapture she might experience over having a rival in the house.

"I'm going to run an antique shop at the Center for Mr. Forbes."

"Working for Mr. Forbes!" Something that in anyone else might pass for eagerness touched her face. "How fortunate for me. But are you terribly brave or are you being foolhardy?"

Blair turned to look at her blankly. "What on earth do you mean?"

"Hasn't anyone told you?" Miss Kenyon exclaimed. "But it's common knowledge, my dear. The man murdered both his wives!"

4

Mr. Potter watched Blair enter the salt box at the Center and then released the brake and drove slowly away. I should have gone in with her, he thought, just to make sure that she and Forbes are going to hit it off. She's an exquisite creature. He ought to be delighted with her. But if he—damn it, I should never have let her come. I knew that at the time. There is no justification for using her as bait. Live bait. And the hell of it is that I can be completely wrong.

He turned onto a dirt road, switched off the motor and lighted a cigarette while he considered the problem of Glen Forbes. They had known each other in college, belonged to the same fraternity, to the same debating society, to the same tennis team. Forbes had been the brilliant one, gay, witty, with a first-rate brain, a delighted laugh that was infectious, and enormous charm. A born leader, they said of him. The man most likely to succeed. The most popular man on the campus.

Yet even then the flaw must have been there, the invisible crack in the structure ready to break at the first strain put on it. Not, Mr. Potter conceded, that the strain had been an easy one to take. To kill a man, whatever the circumstances, was a profound moral shock. And if, as some residue from his childhood, one had an unresolved burden of guilt, however deeply it might be buried—and, according to Kafka, all men carry that burden—the flaw would widen, deepen. The strain that caused the eventual breakage might be trivial in itself.

Glen Forbes had killed the man one night in his senior year. He and Mr. Potter had been returning to college from a week end in New York. Forbes had been at the wheel, driving at a moderate pace. The roads had been nearly free of traffic. Both of them were cold sober. They had stopped at a filling station for gas, a truck had come in, blocking the road so that Forbes had to back out. He had looked automatically in the rearview mirror and put the car in reverse.

It had all happened at once: the truck driver's yell of warning, a man's scream of terror, the sickening lurch when the back wheels went over the body.

No legal action had been taken against Forbes. The filling station attendant, the truck driver and Mr. Potter had all given evidence exculpating him. The man whom Forbes had killed was a drunken derelict who had staggered out of the rest room and approached the car at a stumbling run across an unlighted strip of ground. Apparently he had had some befuddled idea of hitching a ride. He had never been in Forbes' line of vision. So the incident had ended there.

Or begun there. Forbes had sold his car and he never drove again. And he wouldn't discuss the matter. In the first days people had rallied around to say that he was not to blame, but their words seemed to fall on deaf ears. Only once did he make a comment. That was when a misguided friend remarked, "After all, the guy was only a drunken bum."

"So we just exterminate him," Forbes said, "and it won't make any difference." He had gone out of the room. After that, no one mentioned the accident. No one made any remark when he sold his car. Someone always arranged to give him a lift to games and dates. That was the only change. Or if there was any other change in him at the time no one was aware of it.

After college, Forbes and Mr. Potter entered different branches of the Armed Services and lost touch. Then, ten days ago, Glen Forbes had appeared at the Gramercy Park house.

For the first time in their acquaintance they had talked cautiously. Mr. Potter, aware that Forbes must have read newspaper accounts of the murders that had centered in his house a year before, thought he knew the reason for Forbes' deliberate omission of the inevitable questions one asks after a lapse of years. What he could not figure out was why Forbes had come at all.

The small talk ran in a trickle, then in drops, then dried up altogether. Mr. Potter was tempted to let it die on its feet, to compel Forbes to come to the point; but he was, to his cost, a kindly man who suffered an almost physical malaise at the awareness of anyone else's discomfort.

"Whatever became of that attractive girl you used to bring up to dances?" he inquired. "Fannie—Sallie—Connie—Connie Brooks, wasn't it?"

The cold light eyes swept his face. "Yes, Connie Brooks. I married her."

"She was charming. We always foretold you would be lucky."

Forbes caught his breath in a gasp. "She died a few months after we were married."

"I'm awfully sorry. I didn't know, of course."

"It didn't reach the New York papers," Forbes told him. "Neither did the other one." As Mr. Potter's brows arched he said, "The death of my second wife."

He might have been discussing some trivial item of news. "One advantage of money and being a big frog in a little pond is that the local papers don't say things you won't like." His breathing was uneven as though he had been running. "You see, they both died the same way. They killed by hit-run drivers. In fact, there's a growing body of opinion that I did it myself, that I murdered both girls. Not that anyone has said so to me. Sometimes I wish to God they would."

For a moment the man's inhuman control broke. His voice rose. "If they'd just come out and accuse me of murder I could deal with it—in one way or another. What is breaking me down is this silent treatment." He lowered his voice. "Sorry to introduce a note of melodrama."

"Don't be an ass," Mr. Potter said.

"You must be wondering why I came to you with it. I'll clear that part up right away. I came because I knew damned well that you ran into a mess of your own last year and cleared it up."

"But actually I—"

Forbes ignored the startled interruption. "And there's another reason. You were there. You know the death of that drunk when I was in college was an accident. I couldn't help it."

"No one ever said you could," Mr. Potter reminded him mildly.

"They are saying it now. Not straight out to me. In a way that's the damnable part. Like trying to fight a cobweb, like pulling on a slack rope. There's nothing to grapple with. Nothing tangible to get hold of. But little by little the thing has snowballed. I must have gone around in a fog. I didn't know a thing about it. Oh, there were people who acted odd, stared at me as though I had left my other head at home, made remarks that had no particular sense that I could see. Then my family started treating me like an invalid, kind and protective. When it hit me square between the eyes was when I planned to open a pet project of mine, the Bridgetown Center, and found I could get no one, but no one, to work for me. They all had different excuses but they all had the same reason. No mistaking it. They were afraid of me. So then I knew."

The polite code by which Mr. Potter had been brought up provided no tactful phrases for dealing with a man who tells you he is accused of being a murderer. In the past year, however, Mr. Potter had discovered a world in which his polite code was unavailing, a world where one learned to accept the impossible. Because he had succeeded in bearing the unbearable he was not the man he had been a year before. And though he regretted his lost illusions he would not have turned back the clock if he could have done so.

The changes in himself, surprising as he had found them, were nothing compared to the changes in Glen Forbes. In him something had come alive; in Forbes something had died. No, Mr. Potter corrected himself, it had not died but had been muzzled, stamped down, submerged. He shot a troubled glance at the expressionless face. There was enough emotion seething underneath to blow the man sky high.

"What about the local police?"

"They investigated both—deaths as a matter of routine. But at the time there was no suggestion that it wasn't just a tragic coincidence that Connie and Evelyn had died the same way. Killed by hit-run drivers. Except to me, of course. From the very first it had seemed like a kind of retribution."

Mr. Potter was more and more troubled. "For God's sake," he protested, "if you are going to be maudlin—"

Forbes grinned faintly. "Okay. You know what I like about you, Potter, is that in a mad sort of way you have commonsense. It's very inspiriting when one begins getting—fancies."

"Commonsense," Mr. Potter said sadly, "is the kind of quality for which I am always given full credit. I appear to have all the drearier virtues."

Some of the tension went out of Forbes. "Of course, when Evelyn, my second wife, was killed people talked about the coincidence. Two wives killed in the same way, each within a few months of marriage. But until a few weeks ago there wasn't a hint of anything else, anything worse. Then the thing hit me all at once. It's—Potter, you can't imagine what it is like to go around and see in people's faces that they think you are a cold-blooded murderer. To have people watch you, weigh your words, clutch at their wives and daughters if you so much as speak to them on the street—"

Mr. Potter was deeply perplexed. Only a fool could fail to see that Forbes was close to the breaking point. The situation as he outlined it was enough to break any man but there was more behind it, something Forbes was holding back. A rumor as ugly as this one did not gain a foothold unless (a) there was some evidence to support it or (b) someone was working hard to keep it alive. In either case Forbes must inevitably know more than he was telling.

"Have you made any enemies?"

"I don't really know," Forbes admitted. "A man probably never thinks he has an enemy unless he exploits his employees, or beats his children or fights with his neighbors. Unless he's in politics, of course. Though no one can hew to the line he believes in against prevailing opinion and not stir up some opposition."

"What line are you hewing to?"

The question took Forbes by surprise. There was irritation in his voice as he said, "You haven't changed a bit. You still go off on the damnedest, most irrelevant tacks."

"In this case," Mr. Potter pointed out, "we don't know what is relevant. What seems obvious is that either out of malice or something worse, someone is busy circulating a devastating and vicious rumor. You ought to be the best judge of who would be likely to do a thing like that, who would have reason to hit at you, whose toes you have stepped on."

Forbes got up to pace the room, his compact body as full of power as a steam engine. Too much energy there, Mr. Potter thought uneasily.

"Here's the situation," Forbes said, "but if you can show me how it ties into—what it could have to do with stirring people up, not letting those poor girls rest in peace, planting the idea that they were killed deliberately—"

He fell silent while he marshaled his facts and Mr. Potter watched with the patience he had acquired while waiting for his mother's elderly friends to play the next bridge card. There had been nothing in his bland face then to reveal exasperation; there was nothing now to betray startled speculation.

Still pacing up and down the room, his blunt chin outthrust, Forbes began to talk. Watching him, wondering how any one endowed with his extraordinary charm, that quality which had made everyone acknowledge his leadership, could become this tortured creature, repressed to the danger point, Mr. Potter followed only vaguely his first few words.

He had, Forbes said, been born in Bridgetown. He loved the place and wanted to help it maintain its individuality and at the same time its self-sufficiency. The industries were moving away, with resultant unemployment. As assets they had only a few dairy farms and some of the most enchanting scenery in America.

A local guy who had come into some money decided to purchase a big tract of land and turn it into a real estate development. A stereotyped housing project, jerrybuilt but exclusive. No foreigners. No Jews. No children—if possible. Not from any basic dislike of children but because, if they were to be educated, someone would have to pay school taxes. And people seem to prefer to have someone else do that.

Forbes went on rapidly. "Well, I beat him to the draw and bought the property so there would be no part of my community with a 'keep out' sign on it, and at the same time stimulate local handicrafts in a way that would make the people self-supporting, independent of migrating industries. He's sore as a boiled owl, of course. But he wouldn't—he couldn't be back of this thing."

"Why not?"

"Because he is my first wife's uncle, Paul Brooks. He knows damned well I couldn't have—hurt Connie. And what would he gain? She left him what money she had because he was her only relation and I wanted it that way. I didn't need it."

"How much?" Mr. Potter asked.

"Three hundred thousand or thereabouts after taxes. But that isn't the point," Forbes said impatiently.

"What is the point?"

"The point is that I can't live like this. It's a nightmare. There must be some way to clear up this business."

"You mean—find out how your wives died?"

"But there's no mystery about that," Forbes exploded. "They were both killed by hit-run drivers. What I want to know is who is stirring up this witches' broth."

"What you want is a trained detective, a private investigator."

"I even tried that," Forbes told him, "but he didn't get anywhere."

"Who was he? A New York man?"

"He was useless," Forbes said quickly. "He couldn't persuade anyone in the village to talk. Of course, an outsider can't."

"Sure you got hold of a good man?"

Forbes shrugged. "I suppose he was all right."

"What's the agency?"

"Forget him. He couldn't turn up a thing of any value. Look here, Potter, I'm desperate. Come up to Bridgetown yourself, will you, and look around?"

"Look around as how?"

"Anyhow," Forbes said recklessly.

"What do you expect me to do that a trained investigator failed to do?" Mr. Potter asked.

"Get people to talk, for one thing. You always were a darb at that. Find out who is gunning for me—and why."

Mr. Potter was silent.

Forbes watched him for a moment and then turned abruptly toward the door. "Sorry," he said, "it hadn't occurred to me that you would have any doubts."

"Why don't you want me to talk to your detective?"

The two men eyed one another warily and then Forbes capitulated. "His name is Kurt Tyson. You'll find him in the New York telephone directory. Office on Broadway. Ask him anything you damned please. I'll call and clear it with him."

Mr. Potter wrote down the name, ignoring the furious anger smoldering in Forbes. "Do I know you when I go up to Bridgetown or do I just prowl around like a tourist?"

The anger faded. For a moment Forbes relaxed, the old delighted smile appearing on his face. "Matter of fact," he confessed, half amused, half apologetic, "I've been laying a trap for you. Do you remember Mrs. Stanley Brenning?"

"Do I not! An old friend of my mother's. She used to come down occasionally and bring her daughter Joan. They stayed here at the house."

"Her husband is my lawyer and, incidentally, about the only person outside my family who believes in me. The Brennings were dining with me one night not long ago and looking over some old photographs. Found one of you. I gave you quite a build-up. Mrs. Brenning has just one mission in life, to marry off her daughter to a rich man. I told her all I could remember about the Potter fortune. She is planning to ask you to Bridgetown for a nice long visit."

Mr. Potter moaned. "You're an unscrupulous fellow," he complained. "I can see it now: squiring Joan around, playing cutthroat bridge and having nice cosy talks about lonely bachelors and the advantages of matrimony and what a dear home-loving girl Joan is. However, that would probably be as painless a way as any of being on the scene."

Forbes shook his head guiltily. "I've played you a very dirty trick. The woman is a cannibal. You'll never stand a chance."

"You underestimate me," Mr. Potter said mildly.

II

In retrospect he wondered whether he hadn't overestimated himself. To begin with, he had made the appalling blunder of getting Blair Masters the job with Forbes. The latter had said he was searching for someone in New York and she had appeared on the heels of the desperate man, with the qualifications he needed. She had been right for the job, right in every way. Live bait, Mr. Potter thought again, and he hadn't even warned her.

True, he had made the arrangements before his disturbing talk with Kurt Tyson, but there had been time afterwards to call them off, to tell Blair the job had been filled, to send a telegram canceling his visit to Mrs. Stanley Brenning, which had followed hard on Forbes' call.

The detective had not been available until the day before Mr. Potter left New York. He was a smooth, amiable looking man in his mid-fifties, inconspicuously but well dressed. His voice was deceptively bland. Only his eyes were hard, disillusioned.

He had studied Mr. Potter with interest and some surprise. "I've heard of you," he said cryptically. "Got a way of stirring things up, apparently." He looked as though it weren't apparent at all.

"Forbes telephoned to say you might be coming in and to give you what I have." He shuffled some papers on his desk, stared again at Mr. Potter as though seeking the answer to an enigma. "Which isn't much. I went up there to nose around but the people wouldn't open up to me. They clam up with outsiders. Though, like small-town people everywhere, they talk enough among themselves."

"Then you didn't learn anything," Mr. Potter commented.

Again the hard eyes studied him. "Well, I did and I didn't. I scouted around a bit and checked on the deaths of the two Mrs. Forbes. One thing was clear enough. Someone has his knife in Forbes and is working hard to stir up a lot of mud. But who it is——" He emptied an ashtray into his wastebasket, straightened the papers and said abruptly, "Forbes called me off, you know."

"What conceivable reason," Mr. Potter asked, "would anyone have for saying that Forbes deliberately killed those two women?"

"Well," the detective drawled, "there's no question in my mind. Someone did."

"Good God!"

"Look, let's not just horse around on this. Forbes marries Connie Brooks, the girl next door, and everything is lovely. Three months later she is killed by a hit-run driver. Okay, that could happen. But three years later he marries again, a girl named Evelyn Harrison. Not his own class at all, girl from the wrong side of the tracks, not even pretty. And—three months later, *three months,* get that—she is killed by a hit-run driver."

He leaned forward, his eyes boring into Mr. Potter's. "So maybe a man's two wives could die the same way, killed by hit-run drivers. Odd but not impossible. But they both die three months after they marry him. That begins to strain my credulity. And—they both get killed while they are walking through the covered bridge. In the memory of local inhabitants no one else was ever killed that way. And that I don't swallow, brother. Those girls were both murdered."

He looked curiously at the silent, shaken Mr. Potter. "I seem to have jolted you. What's your interest in this?"

Forbes, Mr. Potter explained, was an old friend who was being driven crazy by rumors, hints, a growing but intangible body of opinion that he had killed his wives.

The detective nodded. "That's the line he handed me. He wants someone to help clear him. But he calls off the guy who is trained for the job."

"In other words," Mr. Potter said, "you think he did it."

"What would you think? I couldn't smell a single motive for anyone else. No one gained by the deaths of those women. Well—the first one left a nice fat sum of money to her uncle but he certainly couldn't gain anything by the death of the second wife. No one did. Unless—"

Mr. Potter waited.

"Unless," the detective went on, "Forbes himself gained. Money isn't the only motive where husbands and wives are concerned. Suppose he killed his first wife out of jealousy. Then this other girl came around. She knows too much. He keeps her quiet by marrying her and then gets sick of his bargain."

The hard eyes stared at Mr. Potter. "So you're not buying it," he said at length.

Mr. Potter shook his head. "Out of character."

"No one knows that much about anyone else."

"I know that Forbes is far from being a fool. If he had engineered those two deaths he wouldn't have been insane enough to establish such a series of incredible coincidences. A person planning those two deaths wanted the parallel stressed as hard as possible."

"Well, I'm not completely sold on it myself. But I can tell you this, Mr. Potter, I can't find another candidate. I don't miss much that's under my nose. I'm sure I've got the right man but the motive—hell," said Kurt Tyson, "I know how it sounds. But there have been such cases on record. Not many but enough of them."

"What cases?"

"Bluebeard," the detective said. "Go on and laugh."

But Mr. Potter was not laughing.

5

". . . and tomorrow we'll sit down for a nice long talk about your dear mother," Mrs. Brenning declared as she deposited Mr. Potter in a guest suite with the air of triumph of one who has carried a precious vase to safety.

He thought that she had sharpened with the years, nose and chin more pointed, eyes like bayonets. The nervous tick that jerked her mouth and the tendons of her throat was new. Her effort to control it merely increased the tension of her jaw.

He murmured noncommittally. He was not the supine product he had been and if Mrs. Brenning did not know it now she would learn it in the course of time. In a bloodless revolution he had declared his independence of all elderly women who were determined to run his life and, like converts to a new faith, he was more aggressively zealous about his emancipation than those to whom it had long been a familiar phenomenon.

"But tonight," Mrs. Brenning went on brightly, "belongs to you young people. And especially to Joan. I hope I don't spoil her but an only child, you know—"

Mr. Potter knew. He was an only child himself.

"I'm as glad for her sake to have you here as I am for my own. You've always been a *beau ideal* of hers, you know." She laughed conspiratorily. "Not that she says so but she can't fool her old mother."

You, Mr. Potter apostrophized her silently, should have been a marriage broker. The activities of mothers of marriageable daughters appalled him. Ethically, they made the shadiest of confidence men look like knights in shining armor. They played a ferocious game with no holds barred. Like the Madison Avenue boys they fashioned a career of making second-rate products look like the best the market had to offer.

Mrs. Brenning lingered. "One worries so about a young girl," she said vaguely, "with the terrible things that go on in the world. Well," she expelled a long breath, "I'll feel perfectly safe about Joan when she is with you."

This testimonial to his harmlessness was not particularly flattering but Mr. Potter was interested in the fact that his hostess was alarmed about her daughter.

"Now we've found you again," Mrs. Brenning rambled on, "we must not lose touch. Such a pity for people to lose touch. Your dear mother and I were always so close. It wasn't until I was talking to Glen Forbes the other evening—you've known him a long time, haven't you?"

"Since college." So that was what she was waiting for.

"Yes, that's what he said. I suppose you know he has had a great deal of trouble and sorrow."

"So I gathered."

"You've heard about his two wives, of course." This time the tiny bayonets darted at his face.

"He told me. You probably knew them both well."

"I knew his first wife, Connie Brooks, all her life. She was the niece of an old friend of ours. A very attractive girl." She added thoughtfully, "To men."

His brows arched. "Why didn't you like her?"

She looked at him in surprise. "Why—nothing against her. Only perhaps she was not quite the companion I'd choose for Joan. I don't say she'd have been a bad influence, but—innocent young girls. You know how mothers are."

Bringing a Blush to the Cheek of the Young Person, Mr. Potter thought irresistibly. How Podsnapian could one get?

"Well, no, I don't," he said deprecatingly, "never

having been a mother myself. Did you know his second wife?"

Mrs. Brenning, he observed with some amusement, was disappointed. Prepared to have some malicious gossip about Connie wrested from her reluctant lips, she was cheated of her opportunity.

"I met her a few times. Glen was an old friend of ours and naturally I'd be nice to his wife. She was an Evelyn Harrison." The indefinite article achieved the effect of making her an indefinite person. "Not even pretty except in a wistful, washed-out sort of way. No family, of course. I believe Glen had to give a cousin of hers a job down at the Center. Poor as church mice, all the Harrisons. I can't imagine what Glen saw in her. Nobody could. With his money and those virile good looks and the Forbes charm he might have married anyone. Women always find him irresistible. Fatally attractive."

Somehow this phrase struck her as unfortunate. "However," she switched quickly, "your Miss Masters—"

"Not mine. I've just met her."

"But you arranged this job for her."

"Well, she had the qualifications, you know."

"I suppose," Mrs. Brenning said in a tone freighted with meaning, "you know what you are doing. Of course, we're very fond of Glen; Stanley doesn't believe a word of all this gossip. It makes him furious. But she—she's rather pretty, if you like that type."

Mr. Potter grinned at her. "She is extraordinarily pretty and all men like that type."

"I asked her to dinner. As long as you are interested in meeting her landlady, that writing woman, I thought I might as well have them both."

"How gracious of you," Mr. Potter murmured.

Something in his bland tone made her give him a suspicious look. Then, with the reminder that dinner was at seven-thirty and cocktails at seven, she left him alone.

Mr. Potter bathed and dressed with the leisureliness

he loved, although the Brenning guest suite depressed him. It was too reminiscent of his house on Gramercy Park, the same heavy furniture, the same gloomy rugs and draperies, revealing a love of sheer weight for its own reassuring sake. Perhaps Blair Masters could transform his home into a liveable dwelling in the fall. If everything was all right in the fall. Which brought him back full circle.

It occurred to him that he ought to be grateful if everything was all right during the coming evening. What had possessed him to suggest to his hostess that she ask Ann Kenyon to dinner? That demon in him which he could not always repress had taken over. Like Kurt Tyson, the detective, he boggled at coincidence. If the Kenyon woman had come to Bridgetown to write her next book, there was a reason for it, and the sooner that reason was brought out into the light the better for all concerned. What was breaking Glen Forbes was the undercurrents. Mr. Potter intended to clear the air. He told himself this in a virtuous manner and wondered, a trifle guiltily, whether it was true. The few minutes he had spent with Miss Kenyon when he had delivered Blair's luggage had disturbed him. Her inexplicable hostility had struck him like a current of stale air from an unventilated house.

An unpleasant woman, there was no evading the fact. A trifle unbalanced. Why, Mr. Potter asked himself dismally, can't I learn not to meddle? I wish to God she weren't coming to dinner. But some unregenerate quality in him was profoundly curious.

He adjusted his tie, settled his dinner jacket and then stared at his image in the mirror. Exemplary son, he told himself bitterly. The kind of bachelor whom girls are safe with. Not that he yearned to be a Casanova or even a Don Juan. He had no desire to be a menace to Joan Brenning's heart; certainly not to arouse what he was sure Mrs. Brenning would call her baser instincts, if she could recognize any instinct but the purely acquisitive one. None the less, he was extremely bored with being regarded as harmless.

After a moment's search to see whether he could detect a sinister glint in his eye, which failed, he winked at himself, left the guest suite and ran lightly down the stairs. On the broad landing he paused to look around. The house was far larger than it appeared from the outside, built evidently in the late nineties when Gargantuanism carried prestige. There was a huge drawing room, a big library, a billiard room that doubled as a bar and a dining room that would have fitted nicely into Grand Central Station. The furnishings were pure Podsnap.

He followed the curve of the heavily carpeted stairway down to a wide foyer on whose highly polished floor a few oriental rugs were widely scattered, like islands in the Pacific. Somewhere a woman was pleading desperately, "Please—please—please." As his heel struck the bare floor there was a gasp. "Tonight at dinner, then." A telephone was hastily replaced in its cradle.

Whistling softly to announce his presence, he strolled into the library, a massive room, oak-paneled, with alcoves containing small tables, leather chairs and reading lamps. Some eight thousand books were kept behind glass, a kind of bottled culture to be administered cautiously. Logs blazed in a wide fireplace. Over the mantel hung a well-lighted oil painting of Stanley Brenning who, even from that eminence, seemed rather inadequate to his surroundings, although the artist had done his valiant best. The small Van Dyke concealed an indeterminate chin, the gold-rimmed glasses gave a cast of benevolence to shrewd eyes, the pose that revealed Brenning from the waist up disguised the fact that he was only an inch or so over five feet tall.

The only occupant of the room was Joan Brenning, huddled in a big chair beside a telephone stand. To Mr. Potter there seemed to be something pinched about her, something almost haggard in her expression. For a fleeting moment he had an impression that she was looking into the bottomless pit but he had, as he knew, a tendency to be fanciful.

She turned toward the door with the guilty motion of a thief caught in the act, recognized him and sagged in relief. Then she summoned up a smile and ran to him with both hands outstretched in welcome.

"Hiram Potter! How nice. I'm so sorry I missed you when you arrived."

All that clothes could do for her had been done but it had not, Mr. Potter admitted with regret, been enough. The dress of virginal white made her seem too knowing. The soft waves of her blond hair accentuated the sharpness of her features. And yet she came so close to being very pretty, she missed it by so little. She would burn herself out in a few years. She was too tense, too strained, too shrill.

"Drinks are in the billiard room," she said. "I could use one." There was a feverish flush burning under the rouge on her cheekbones. She gave him a conspiratorial grin as she tucked her hand under his arm. "And you'll need one. Brace up and prepare for a shock. Mother has her eye on you and the Potter money for me."

"How flattering," Mr. Potter said amiably.

Her eyes held a touch of her father's shrewdness. She nodded. "I thought so."

"What is that supposed to mean? I am a simple soul. Don't go cryptic on me."

"I just meant I thought mother was off the beam," Joan said candidly. "She usually is, you know. Especially about men. Well, that's all right then." She did not attempt to conceal her relief. "Just play along a bit and it will be easier for both of us."

"Cat's paw Potter they call me. But no tricks."

"Why do you say that?" Joan broke off as her father and mother came in, the former advancing with slow state to shake hands, the latter in black lace and pearls. She looked swiftly from Joan to Mr. Potter, a faint smile denting the corners of her thin lips when she saw Joan's arm linked with that of the young man.

The smile faded as she examined her husband.

"Stanley, I told you to get your hair cut this morning. I can't see why you object to having a valet to keep you in order."

"I can dress myself," Brenning said with the irritation of one answering a familiar complaint. "But I am sorry about the haircut, Beulah. It went entirely out of my mind. This has been rather an upsetting day. Paul Brooks is stirring up a hurricane in the village, trying to call a town meeting about the Center, though what he hopes to accomplish, except to make himself offensive, is beyond me. Anyhow, Forbes got hold of it and instructed me to tear up his will."

"Paul is being provoking," Mrs. Brenning said, rather inadequately, "but I must admit I can't see any tragedy in Glen Forbes changing his will. Think of having all that money and leaving it to the community! I mean it isn't any good to anyone."

An imp of laughter gleamed out of Mr. Potter's eyes and ducked back out of sight.

"Why shouldn't he leave it to his own family?" Mrs. Brenning went on.

"He has a right to dispose of his property as he pleases," her husband remarked. He warned her, "And don't speak of it. Just because I mention it in my own house—"

"I can be discreet," his wife said tartly. "A lot more discreet than you ever are. Men! Just the same, as his lawyer you ought to give Glen a hint. Tell him that no one really gives a person credit for leaving money to a community or to an organization. Either they think he is trying to escape taxes or that he has so much he doesn't know what else to do with it."

"Forbes hasn't any family except for Emily Cook and she inherited as much as he did. She doesn't need it—"

"Or want it," Joan put in. "She's crazy about the idea of the Center and she has begun to rush around talking to farmers' wives about hooking rugs or something like that. Of course, Charlie hasn't a cent to his name except what Glen gives him and heaven knows he could use it."

"It would be wasted on Charlie," Mrs. Brenning said. "It would be like pouring water into a sieve."

At the same moment her husband said, "There's no reason why Charlie shouldn't try to support himself for a change instead of living off Glen."

Joan looked from one to another. "You both hate Charlie's guts, don't you?" She shrugged her thin shoulders and took Mr. Potter into the billiard room, which didn't look much larger than the Yankee Stadium. Unfortunately, its dimensions tended to dwarf rather than to magnify Brenning. Even when all the guests had assembled, the room maintained its air of splendid isolation.

The first to arrive was Charlie Forbes, who came into the room with a faintly defiant swagger, seemingly oblivious to the restrained welcome of his hosts, and kissed Joan, chiefly, Mr. Potter suspected, to annoy the Brennings. Later, he wondered why he had been so sure. It was Charlie's physical likeness to Glen, for which he was unprepared, which most interested him.

Charlie, a careless arm around Joan, shook hands with Mr. Potter. He grinned impudently. "I see the Brennings have set you up as my rival. Watch it, Potter. First thing you know you'll be stuffed like the furniture. This place does things to people." His face stiffened. "Oh, oh. My name's Sir Oracle and when I open my lips let no dog bark. Lead me to a drink, my proud beauty."

Joan called across the bar for another martini for herself and Scotch for Charlie. Mr. Potter glanced toward the doorway to see who had aroused Charlie Forbes's annoyance. The florid, self-assured man in his late forties who had just come in was introduced as Paul Brooks. There was quickened interest in the eyes that surveyed Mr. Potter, an interest to which the latter had become inured if not reconciled in the past year. But the flattering attention which the older man

showed him was owing, he knew, to the Potter money.
Mr. Brenning brought the two men drinks while his
wife hovered near the bar, keeping a watchful eye on
Joan and Charlie Forbes.

In a few moments Emily and Jerome Cook entered
the room with Blair Masters and her landlady, Ann
Kenyon. Emily, vital, forthright and kind, accomplished
the minor miracle of giving the place an air of warmth.
Her stout, bald-headed husband remained in the background except when, to Mr. Potter's amusement, he
periodically checked his wife's unruly tongue and
brought her within bounds.

Blair Masters, as he had realized before, was lovely.
A simple evening dress of violet crepe pointed up the
sheen of her dark hair and the tilt of her eyes. Apparently, Mrs. Brenning had exhausted her hospitality in
extending the invitation, and after a brief greeting left
the girl alone. Jerome Cook turned to her with a smile
and drew her into easy conversation.

It was Miss Kenyon, however, at whom Mr. Potter
looked in consternation. She wasn't a pretty woman
but she was, he thought, dangerous. A woman of
smoldering force with haunted eyes. She wore a shabby
evening dress of dull red velvet with an air. A little
heavy for contemporary fashion, she appeared full bo-
somed and voluptuous. He felt his heart sink.

6

Apparently the martinis were catching up with Joan. Her voice was getting higher, her face more deeply flushed. She had abandoned Charlie Forbes and was clinging to Paul Brooks' arm. He patted her hand with the least convincing imitation of a paternal gesture that Mr. Potter had ever encountered.

The latter gravitated toward Blair, smiling at her awed expression.

"Brobdingnag," she told him in a half whisper. "I didn't know people actually lived in places like this. How do they find their way around without signposts?"

"They ought to do a line in conducted tours," he replied, his voice low.

"How do you communicate with anyone across the room? By smoke signals?"

Miss Kenyon, leaning against the bar, looked sharply from one to the other, her attention caught by that low-toned conversation.

"Room all right?" he asked.

"Just fine," Blair assured him.

"And your landlady?"

"I can't make her out. This afternoon I thought she was negative and dowdy, but look at her now! She has blossomed out—in a gruesome sort of way."

"A night-blooming plant apparently."

Charlie Forbes came up, neatly cut Blair out of the pack and settled her on a wide windowseat with an old-fashioned and a plate of canapes. "Well," he said, "this is more like it. I began to think there was a conspiracy to keep me from knowing you any better, but now I have the situation under control, we're supplied with food and plied with liquor and have a good defensive position."

The engaging grin faded. "Look here, Miss Masters, I hope you didn't take that little blow-up at the Center too seriously. Glen has been under a strain and he lets loose on occasion. But it doesn't mean a thing."

"Of course not."

"Then you'll let me see you now and then? Good!" he exclaimed as though she had agreed. "That's all right, then." His tone changed. "Hold my hand, will you, if you see me losing my temper."

"Why should you lose your temper?"

"Sir Oracle," he muttered.

Paul Brooks was beside them. Joan had left him and moved on to speak to Jerome Cook. Brooks coolly settled himself between Blair and Charlie with every appearance of meaning to stay. Charlie's lips parted in protest and then he turned abruptly away.

Brooks' eyes traveled over Blair's face, lingered on her body. "I understand you are going to live in Bridgetown for a while, Miss Masters. How fortunate for us."

"That's pleasant to hear," she said, thinking what pig-like eyes he had.

"They tell me you are going to devote your talents to the Center. How do you like it?"

"So far I've had time only for a brief glance," she said casually, ignoring the heavy sarcasm in his voice. "But it strikes me as a wonderful idea."

"It strikes you that way, does it? You've fallen for Forbes' propaganda."

"I've just met him. I really don't know him at all."

Brooks gave her a skeptical look, met level eyes, and his tone changed. "He will undoubtedly rectify the situation. Forbes is quite a man with the ladies. Both the Forbes men are. They'll hardly pass up anything as attractive as you. Not two ladies' men like that. Personally, I am a plain businessman. No fol-do-rol and art for the masses. I'd like to help this community grow and thrive and treble its population."

Blair surprised herself by coming to the defense of Glen Forbes' project. "It's wonderful," she declared, "to find a place that is uncrowded and restful."

Brooks' face turned a dark red and Blair wondered whether he suffered from high blood pressure. "Stagnant is the word," he corrected her. "This back-to-the-spinning wheel stuff is archaic. Nothing stands still, Miss Masters. It grows or it dies."

"Still," said Mr. Potter's quiet voice, "there are different kinds of growth." Adroitly he shifted Brooks' attention to himself and Blair found Charlie back at her elbow, grinning like the Cheshire cat.

"Teamwork," he explained as he led her to the bar. "Potter ran interference for me. A very efficient guy, Potter." As the butler announced dinner he muttered, "There goes our chance for a second drink. In the public good, though, that's probably just as well."

"What do you mean?" Blair asked.

"The Kenyon female. Hadn't you noticed? She really laps it up. I see that Jerome is taking her in to dinner. Tactful Jerome will manage her if anyone can. You're my partner, by the way, which is nice for me but a slap at you. In these parts I am definitely regarded as low man." He looked around. "I wonder why Glen didn't come. He can't still be sore at me. Oh, there he is."

Glen Forbes had entered the room and gone directly to his hostess with a murmured apology. Blair found herself staring at him, endeavoring to see him as a man who had murdered two women and found, to her relief, that it could not be done.

"But I could have sent a car for you, Glen," Mrs. Brenning protested. "It's so absurd of you not to have one of your own."

"All that surprises me," Brooks remarked, "is that Forbes doesn't drive a horse and buggy. Let's be consistent at all costs."

So far as Mr. Potter could tell, neither then nor later did Forbes ever glance in Brooks' direction. He ignored him completely. There was a marked hostility between him and his first wife's uncle which he had not mentioned during that talk on Gramercy Park.

"But I thought you had broken down and bought a car," Joan exclaimed. "Whose car were you driving the other night?"

"When was that?" Forbes asked alertly.

"Why Tuesday or Wednesday, I think. Up Route 7 toward Canaan."

"Your mistake," he told her.

"But," she insisted, "I'm sure I recognized—"

"Glen," Emily intervened, "hasn't been behind the wheel of a car to my certain knowledge for more than eight years."

Paul Brooks laughed.

Mr. Potter thought that even without that bit of dialogue, followed as it was by an awkward silence, the dinner would have been doomed from the start. There was no question about where the source of the trouble lay. Paul Brooks was bent on stirring up Forbes; he seemed determined to rouse the terrible temper that Mr. Potter remembered vividly from his college days.

"I see," he remarked, "they have arrested that college kid who knocked down the janitor. About time something like that was done. These privileged youngsters think they can get away with murder. And sometimes they even try that later on."

Forbes' jaw tightened but he made no comment. Charlie looked quickly from one man to the other but Brooks had kept his comment impersonal. To treat it otherwise would only make matters worse. Mrs. Brenning, who apparently did not recognize the glancing blow at Forbes, took up the subject of juvenile delinquency and laid down the law in regard to its treatment, punishment and cure in a manner that involved the use of every cliché on the subject.

When she had run down, Brooks addressed Mr. Potter. "Have you inspected our local project yet? You'll have to ask Forbes to explain it. About all I can make out is that he is giving the community several million dollars—for reasons best known to himself."

Glen Forbes might have been deaf. He went on stolidly eating his dinner. "Some people," Charlie exploded, "like giving about as much as you like getting, Brooks. You wouldn't understand that."

Forbes caught Charlie's eye across the table. "Drop it," he advised.

No, on the whole it was not a successful dinner. Charlie was on the verge of flying at Brooks' throat and Forbes remained silent. Jerome Cook was doing his valiant best to entertain Miss Kenyon who, as became increasingly apparent to everyone but Emily Cook, was drunk. Her face was flushed and her eyes were glazed. She was preternaturally dignified but the effect was marred by spasmodic hiccups that came out in little explosions.

So it was Emily the kindly who precipitated the catastrophe. Emily, in an effort to switch attention away from the hostility between Paul Brooks and the Forbes men, turned to Miss Kenyon.

"We are so proud," she said, "to find that our community has something to offer a writer, even if it is just peace and quiet."

"Stagnation," Brooks said clearly.

"Oh, Paul," she implored him with a pleading gesture, "please, don't. Anyhow, a writer can find inspiration here. I'm sure Miss Kenyon will agree."

"I didn't come for inspiration," Miss Kenyon said in a thick voice.

We've got to stop her, Mr. Potter thought in alarm. He broke in. "I've always wondered whether a professional writer really does rely on inspiration. I recall a friend of—"

Having taken the bit in her teeth, Miss Kenyon was not to be checked. "I came here to collect material for my new book."

"Material about a moribund community," Forbes put in and Mr. Potter wondered whether he was deliberately baiting her.

Miss Kenyon had had enough liquor to release her inhibitions. "Rot," she said crudely. "Material about murder."

Mrs. Brenning pushed her chair back hastily. "We'll have coffee in the drawing room." Her guests got to their feet but Miss Kenyon imperviously remained seated.

"Murder!" Her voice rose. "The unforgivable sin against society. Everywhere. Top to bottom. Prince to pauper. The men who butcher women and sometimes get away with it because society allows them to do it. But they must be smoked out. The world must see the modern Bluebeards in all their horror. They must be punished."

"But why Bridgetown?" Joan asked, ignoring her mother's frantic signals.

"Because the crimes were here."

"Stanley," Mrs. Brenning said desperately, "can't you do something? Emily, Joan, Miss Masters—coffee in the drawing room, please." The last word was practically a bleat.

"Really, Miss Kenyon," Brenning said, flustered, "you must not—as a lawyer I must advise you—without evidence—"

Miss Kenyon tried to focus her eyes on him. "I was brought here to find the evidence. Nothing can shtop me." She reached for her wine glass, overturned it and looked stupidly at the spreading stain, her head lolling.

Mr. Potter materialized at her elbow, drew out her chair, got her to her feet and dragged her across the room. "I'll take her home," he said without checking his rapid progress toward the door, firmly steering the woman.

"Give the witch some arsenic while you are about it," Charlie advised loudly. "If she's got anything more to say I'll cram her teeth down her throat."

"That will do, Charlie!" Forbes grasped his arm and caught Mrs. Brenning's eye. "Afraid we had better break up the party." As Charlie tried to twist away he tightened his grip. "You are coming with me. Tomorrow you'll make your apologies."

"I'm tired of being pushed around," Charlie said.
"Through with it. You'll find out." He added defiantly,
"And I am taking Miss Masters home."

"I must go with Miss Kenyon," Blair explained.
"Mr. Potter will need help with her."

The hapless Brennings stood watching their dinner
party disintegrate. Only Paul Brooks appeared to be
enjoying himself. Emily hovered in distress between
him and the Forbes men, her presence serving as a
kind of shield to deflect their hostility. Joan shrugged
her shoulders and began to talk to Jerome Cook.

When Blair came down the stairs with her evening
wrap the front door stood open and everyone was outside. A motor started up in the big oval driveway. Mr.
Potter came to her.

"My car is down at the end. You'll have to sit in
back. I've got your landlady in front."

A bright light blinded Blair, someone screamed, Mr.
Potter jerked her violently to one side.

"All right?" he asked.

"Yes." She clung to his arm and said absurdly, "I
lost my slipper."

He was grim. "There it is."

It lay in the driveway, crushed by a tire. Just
beyond, Charlie's car came to a grinding stop. Both the
Forbes men leaped out and ran toward her.

"Are you hurt?" Forbes asked.

Blair shook her head. "Just frightened."

Charlie, a queer blank look in his eyes, stood staring
at her. He said nothing at all.

Mr. Potter bent over to retrieve the slipper, its satin
split, its heel broken. Forbes took it from him and
turned it over and over, his face gray. No one spoke or
moved.

Then Emily was at his side, her hand on his arm.
"Glen," she said gently.

"Wait," her husband blundered. "We don't even
know that Glen was driving."

"Just another accident," Brooks sneered.

Mr. Potter turned to Blair. "Can you walk?"

"If I hang on to you. I'm lopsided with only one slipper."

She limped beside him to the big yellow convertible. In the front seat Miss Kenyon slept, oblivious to the excitement. Mr. Potter drove in silence through the covered bridge, down the dirt road to the brown cottage.

When he had put Miss Kenyon down on her bed he stood looking at her.

"I expect I'd better get her clothes off," Blair said at last.

"No, just let her alone. She's not likely to wake up." He took Blair into the living room.

"Well," she said, letting out her breath in a long sigh.

"Call me anything you want to," Mr. Potter said in contrition. "Have hysterics. Sue me. Tomorrow I'll take you back to New York and give you my personal check for your summer—and still owe you a debt."

"That's silly. But I do think it's time you told me what this is all about. Miss Kenyon said Mr. Forbes murdered both his wives by running over them. What is he supposed to be—some kind of maniac? Did he deliberately try to kill me tonight?"

The words sounded so monstrous that she added, "I simply don't believe it."

"Actually," Mr. Potter said, "I'm not sure which man was driving that car."

7

"I should never have let you come," Mr. Potter declared. "Even when we first discussed it, I knew there might be a risk."

Blair clasped her hands together hard to stop their trembling. "It's about time you tell me what this is all about, don't you think?"

He gave her a look of mingled guilt and contrition. "I'm not sure what it is all about."

In spite of her upset state, or perhaps because of it, Blair found herself laughing. The sight of Mr. Potter's subdued expression changing to one of alarm increased her hilarity. She rocked back and forth. At length she pulled herself together.

"Sorry," she said, "I didn't mean to let go like that, but you looked so meek in such," her voice quavered again, "in such a demented sort of way." She wiped her eyes. "Well, I feel better now, not so shaky. Look here, I don't know what you are playing at but I'd better explain that I overheard Mr. Forbes at your house. I recognized his voice as soon as I heard it today. He said something about people accusing him of murder. This afternoon Miss Kenyon told me it was common knowledge that he had killed both his wives. And tonight—" she began to shiver again.

"Yes, tonight. That really puts the lid on it." There was nothing demented about Mr. Potter's manner now. "And yet, Miss Masters, we simply can't attach too much meaning to that near-accident tonight. It must have been sheer carelessness. A meaningless business." He caught her eye and added hastily, "Though it might have been unpleasant for you."

"Considering," she said bluntly, "that if you hadn't jerked me out of the way when you did, I'd have been run over, I consider that the understatement of the week. Now, please tell me what's wrong. There were so many undercurrents at that beastly dinner party that I've never sat through a more ghastly meal. What's wrong here?"

"It's a queer story. One that goes back to college." Mr. Potter started with the accidental death of the drunken derelict, went on to Forbes' visit to him in New York and concluded with the report he had received from Kurt Tyson, the detective whom Forbes had hired and then dismissed.

For a moment he listened at the door of Miss Kenyon's room, where her heavy breathing indicated that she was fast asleep. He came back, glanced at Blair and knelt to lay a fire. When the logs caught, he drew her chair closer to the blaze.

"Well, there it is, and anything you may be thinking of me at this moment for dragging you into it is quite justified."

"After all," Blair reminded him quietly, "I practically forced you to do it."

He shook his head. "I did it partly, I suppose, because Forbes was looking for someone with your qualifications and you cropped up at the psychological moment, needing a job. You have probably guessed that the local people are afraid to work for him."

She nodded.

"And partly because—well, call it a hunch. Understand, I don't dismiss the possibility that Forbes is guilty; obviously, the detective thought so. That's why Forbes didn't want me to talk to him. But somehow I don't think he is. It occurred to me—" he looked uneasily at Blair and his voice dwindled off.

"Go on," she said.

"Well, you are an extremely attractive young woman and—"

"As the third Mrs. Forbes I might test the Kenyon Bluebeard theory."

He was horrified. "Not as bad as that. Naturally I didn't expect you to marry him. But I thought if he revealed an interest in you and there was someone who didn't want him to marry—"

Unexpectedly Blair laughed. "You know, Mr. Potter, you are a very dangerous man. But why should anyone object to his marrying? You mean a jealous woman?"

"I don't know what I mean," he confessed. "I'm floundering. So far as I can see, no one has gained by the deaths of those two women. Well, Paul Brooks gained by his niece's death. Evelyn, however, had no money. Anyhow, Forbes himself certainly didn't profit. Unless—"

"Well?"

"Unless," he said reluctantly, "killing that derelict did something to him. He said something about the deaths of his wives, killed as they were, being a form of retribution. We can't dismiss the idea that he has got a kink of some sort. A dangerous kink. It's not a pleasant possibility."

The warmth of the fire had reached her now and she had stopped trembling. The panic fear which had shaken her when she had so nearly been run over was gone, but she was tense, over-alert. Oddly enough, she found herself thinking not of the immediate problem but of Dr. Evans' warning. He, too, had mentioned Bluebeard.

Color mounted into her face and Mr. Potter, watching her, wondered what had caused it. She looked at him and saw the question in his eyes.

"I was thinking," she said slowly, "that I've heard more about Bluebeard today than since I was a little girl playing, 'Sister Ann, Sister Ann, do you see anyone coming?' Here's Miss Kenyon—"

"Damn Miss Kenyon," Mr. Potter said fervently. "And, by the way, that settles it. You go home tomorrow. It's bad for you to have to walk through that covered bridge to work. It's worse to have you subjected to another accident. But it's completely impossible if that woman is a dipsomaniac."

"Well, if you think so—just a minute!" Blair sat bold upright. "If I dash off to New York after that near-accident tonight, that will really put the lid on it for Mr. Forbes, won't it?" When he remained silent she repeated, "Won't it? By tomorrow everyone in the village would think that he is a homicidal maniac."

"There is no reason why you should consider that," Mr. Potter told her. "After all, this isn't your responsibility."

"Anything I do that could have so vicious an effect is my responsibility," Blair said quietly.

Mr. Potter brightened. "Good girl. Of course, you needn't stay long, just a few days until we can work out a convincing excuse for you, something that won't seem to point the finger of suspicion at Forbes."

"Then you do believe in him."

"I want to," he admitted. "So far, all I know is that an evil brew is being stirred up here. Right now the focal point seems to be Paul Brooks. That conversation tonight, for instance—"

"The college boy who struck the janitor!" Blair exclaimed. "At the time I didn't see—"

"The college boy," Mr. Potter agreed. "He's trying to hammer home the fact that Forbes is a killer. But there are a lot of other things. For instance, the fact that Joan Brenning insists that she saw Forbes driving a car and he declares that he does not drive. The fact that there is a deep hostility between the two Forbes men. Charlie, by the way, seems to have a bad reputation on the whole, both in regard to money and to women. The fact that Miss Kenyon came here to do a Bluebeard book and made obvious that Forbes was her target. The fact that Joan Brenning—did you get the impression that she was particularly interested in any one of the men tonight?"

"All men," Blair said dryly. "Any man."

Mr. Potter, remembering Joan's anguished pleading over the telephone, wondered which of the men at the dinner party was the one to whom she had talked, the one to whom she had said so desperately, "Please—please—please." "Of course," he said aloud, "I'll have to check on Forbes having a car. The two cousins are so much alike that, if any funny business is going on, I'd lay ten to one it is Charlie. What baffles me is the motive behind all this. No one profits by discrediting Forbes. Even if the idea is to get him convicted of murder, no one would inherit. His only beneficiary is the community—or, look, he is intestate now!"

"I know," Blair said. "I was at the Center when Charlie came in with some story about Paul Brooks intending to warn the community that the whole project of the Center was a sort of bribe. Mr. Forbes was so angry that he instructed Mr. Brenning to destroy his will."

"Charlie again," Mr. Potter said thoughtfully. "But I gathered that Forbes wouldn't leave anything to him in any case."

"Mr. Forbes was furious when Charlie offered to drive me home from the Center," Blair said. "He thinks he is a dangerous driver. Could he possibly suspect that Charlie killed those women? No, it can't be that. They must be friends because I heard Charlie thank him for making a deposit—oh, there's something I forgot!"

She told him about George Harrison's defalcations and how the accountant had warned Forbes to let it go.

Harrison, Mr. Potter explained, was a cousin of Forbes' second wife, Evelyn Harrison. So far as he could make out, Forbes had had bad luck with both wives. There was gossip to be picked up about Connie. As for Evelyn, the only mystery seemed to be why he had married her at all.

He got up again to listen at Miss Kenyon's door. "Are you sure," he asked, "that you can take her?"

"I can try. If she is impossible I can stay with the Cooks. But what a strange coincidence that she should have come here to write a book about a murderer!"

"Coincidence!" Mr. Potter ejaculated. "Remember, I told you that you weren't as intelligent as you thought. You're not even as intelligent as I thought. But much more attractive." This last thought seemed to bring him little comfort. "Well, I'll keep an eye on you and at the first sign of anything wrong, run screaming."

Blair laughed. "I don't know of any more stimulating last words. But I'll be all right and, I'll say this for you, Mr. Potter, you pick interesting jobs. At least, I won't be bored." She leaned back in her chair and kicked off her remaining slipper.

Mr. Potter pulled its torn mate out of his pocket and set it beside the other. "There are worse things than boredom," he commented.

Blair found herself shivering again as she remembered the blinding light, the scream of brakes, the jerk with which Mr. Potter had pulled her out of the path of the car.

"There's one strange fact about your landlady," he said. "Who tipped her off? There hasn't been a syllable in any newspaper to indicate that Forbes had anything to do with the hit-run killing of his two wives. Not a hint of murder. So—who told her? Well, I'll see what I can find out about the woman."

"Couldn't I do that more easily than you?" Blair asked suddenly. "She hates men. She'd never talk to you. And she made clear that she expects me to be a source of information to her, passing on anything I learn on my job. If there's anything in reciprocity—"

"Hates men!" Mr. Potter shook his head. "No, Miss Masters, no! Haven't you looked at the woman? She is endowed with more than her share of sex. It isn't hate she feels; it's fear. Be careful about questioning her. Don't let her see what you are after."

"You make me feel as though I'd settled in a snake pit," Blair commented. "And yet if it hadn't been for that accident tonight, I'd find all this impossible to believe. But why—why try to kill me? It simply must have been an accident! It has to be. Mr. Forbes—"

"I told you," Mr. Potter said, 'that I didn't see which of the Forbes men was at the wheel."

"Charlie is the one who is accident prone. At least, that is what Mrs. Cook says."

"What do you think of the Forbes family?" Mr. Potter asked her.

"I like Emily Cook immensely. Charlie—" she hesitated. "He's engaging and good company but rather unpredictable, I'd say."

"And Forbes?"

Blair hesitated longer. "I don't know," she admitted. She looked up to find Mr. Potter studying her with a troubled expression. To her own annoyance she felt the hot blood sweep over her face and she was powerless to control it.

"And Paul Brooks?" Mr. Potter seemed to be unaware of her confusion.

"A prosperous traveling salesman with a roving eye."

"A roving eye," Mr. Potter said alertly. "I hadn't noticed."

"Any woman would," Blair assured him. "Piggy little eyes that take your clothes off."

"Well, well."

"But he's more than that. Obviously he's the man who is stirring up the rumors. What I wonder is why he has suddenly come out in the open."

"So do I," Mr. Potter admitted. "And what do you think of Jerome Cook?"

She laughed softly. "The poor man is so busy keeping his wife out of trouble—but what a darling she is!"

"You're sure you want to go on with this?" As Blair nodded, Mr. Potter said, "Well, then, we can try it for a week. But you realize, of course, that you'll have to walk through that covered bridge twice a day."

"That's why Emily Cook was afraid!" Blair summoned up a shaky smile. "I've always rather liked covered bridges."

II

And what, she wondered while she undressed, made me say that? Why didn't I jump at his offer to send me back to New York and pay for the summer? Before she could formulate an answer that satisfied her she fell asleep.

It seemed like a few minutes, although it was nearly four o'clock, when she awakened. At first, having become accustomed to the shifting reflection of headlights across her ceiling at night, the darkness baffled her. There were no traffic noises; only the sound of the river running over stones. She remembered then where she was. But what had awakened her?

Then she became aware of the sounds from the next room. For a moment she was tempted, in her disgust, to go back to sleep and let Miss Kenyon cope with her own nausea. But you can't, she decided, let a fellow creature remain without help, so she got out of bed, put on robe and slippers, groped for the light switch and opened the bathroom door.

When Miss Kenyon had finished retching, Blair helped her back to her room, undressed her with considerable difficulty and got her into bed. She opened the window wide. Then, seeing the eyes fixed on her face she drew up a chair beside the bed.

"Better now?"

Miss Kenyon nodded. "Something I ate. I have a very sensitive stomach. Sorry to be so much trouble on your first night. Will you—would you mind leaving the light on?"

Blair was aware that the other woman was afraid of the dark, afraid to be alone with her sick fancies, her alcoholic thoughts.

"I'm not sleepy," she lied. "Do you want to talk for a while?" She was rewarded by the look of gratitude on that ravaged face.

"It's funny," Miss Kenyon said, "the things a person is afraid of. With me it's darkness. I always keep a light burning at night. Even as a child. Especially as a child. So I could see if anyone was there and what he was doing. But here in the country it's as black as pitch. No traffic. No neighbors within call. Nothing."

"It doesn't seem so bad to me," Blair said. "I'm a small-town girl myself. Used to dark nights. But if you've always lived in a city it will take time to become adjusted."

"I'm small-town myself. Elmwood, New York."

"How did you happen to discover Bridgetown?" Blair asked casually. "It's so out of the way."

"I go where my work takes me. I'd been looking for a new subject and found there was one here."

"One what?"

"Wife killer." Miss Kenyon stretched out a hand that was cold and clammy and clutched at Blair's arm. "Tell me what you find out about Mr. Forbes," she said avidly.

"Miss Kenyon," Blair said slowly and distinctly, "you must not write such a book about a living man. No publisher would dare bring it out. Mr. Forbes would win a libel suit that could drive the firm out of business."

"I'll change the locality and the name, naturally. I know what I'm doing."

"But after what you said at dinner tonight people would know whom you meant."

"What did I say?" She hauled herself up on her pillow. Her face had a smudged look. Her eyelids were puffy.

"That you had come here to get material on murder."

Miss Kenyon blinked at her. "Would you be kind enough to bring me a glass of water?"

Blair looked in the bathroom, found no glass, went to the kitchen and filled a glass with water. She held Miss Kenyon's head while she sipped it.

"Can I get you anything else?" she asked. "Some aspirin to help you sleep?"

Miss Kenyon shook her head. "I don't believe in

drugs. I never take anything. What were we talking about?"

"About how you happened to come here."

"That's funny. I never knew until tonight which—whist—witch one—" her voice blurred, thickened. "He was scared when he saw that I'd guessed." She turned on her side and slept.

Blair left the light burning and went wearily back to bed. The night air was chilly and she pulled blankets over her bare shoulders, shivering. For a moment she watched the crack of light from Miss Kenyon's room and then she fell asleep.

When she was aroused by the alarm clock in the morning she stumbled out of bed, dressed in a rust-colored cardigan and brown tweed skirt and went into the kitchen where she measured out coffee, boiled an egg and made toast. She peered into Miss Kenyon's room, saw the blotched face, heard her heavy breathing, and drew back in distaste.

But when she was out of doors and saw light clouds scudding through the sky, the river sparkling in the sunlight, mountain laurel coming into bloom, she drew a long breath and walked briskly down the dirt road toward the covered bridge.

It was true, as she had told Mr. Potter, that she liked covered bridges but she found herself hesitating at the entrance. She peered through the gloom to the other end and, once inside, she raced at top speed through it, in a panic lest a car trap her there. When she emerged breathless she stopped to look down at the river and fill her laboring lungs. Don't ever do that again, she told herself. After all, it happened only to Glen Forbes' wives.

At first she thought the Center was deserted. Then she saw smoke curling from the chimney of the little white salt box. She peered through the windows but the two offices on the first floor were empty. She lifted the shiny brass knocker.

Glen Forbes clattered down the circular staircase and opened the door. He looked at her in surprise.

"Come up, won't you? I live upstairs." He stood back to let her precede him up the stairs to a small but charming living room with logs burning in a white fireplace. He waved her to a chair and slipped on his coat.

On a pine bench in front of the fire was a coffee cup and an outsize ashtray that held a smoldering cigarette.

Blair hung back. "I'm so sorry. I've interrupted your breakfast. You didn't tell me what time you expected me."

"I didn't expect you," he said. "After last night I thought you wouldn't be staying."

8

When he had left Blair, Mr. Potter got thoughtfully into the rakish yellow convertible. At the entrance to the covered bridge he stopped. His headlights illuminated it from end to end, from side to side. Because the approach at either end was on a steep curve no one could enter it at high speed. Certainly no driver could miss seeing anything the size of a bird that moved in it. Kurt Tyson had been right, of course. The two women had been run down deliberately.

He went on through the bridge. There were no lights in the Center. If Forbes had returned home he had already gone to bed. Mr. Potter drove up the hill to the Brenning house and was grateful to find that here, too, there were no signs of life. In his own room he took off his coat, tie and shoes, made himself comfortable in dressing gown and slippers, and sat brooding over a cigarette.

Why had Glen Forbes come to him for help? Because, he claimed, Mr. Potter had succeeded in unraveling his own mystery. Which was not accurate. The police had done that. Mr. Potter, as he was well aware, had been on the wrong track from beginning to end. About the only purpose his intervention had served had been to make things happen; to act, in Blair Masters' words, as a catalytic agent.

Then why dismiss a trained detective and turn to an untrained amateur? Because Kurt Tyson believed Forbes had killed his wives. Bluebeard, he had said, defying Mr. Potter to laugh. Mr. Potter had not laughed then. He did not laugh now.

He considered, with as much detachment as he could summon up, the possibility that Forbes had developed a dangerous mania after the accidental death of the tramp, that he had become a compulsive killer. "Retribution," Forbes had said, referring to the deaths of his wives. A kind of divine punishment. When a man began thinking in those terms there was trouble ahead.

The problem of Glen Forbes' sanity was outside Mr. Potter's orbit. If necessary, he would find a specialist who could deal with it. His own task was a humbler one, dealing with tangible facts. The car, for instance. If Forbes had killed his wives he must have had access to a car. Tyson could hardly have failed to check on that and the local police would have found tire marks or traces of some kind. Not, of course, that such evidence would be likely to help now, three years after the death of the second wife.

Forbes claimed that he had not driven since he was in college, and his sister backed him. Thinking of Emily Cook, Mr. Potter found himself smiling. She was a thoroughly nice woman and not a fool. Not the sentimental kind who would let her judgment be blinded by her affections. There was a lot of character under that engaging warmth of manner.

The smile conjured up by Emily faded as he considered Joan Brenning's claim that she had seen Forbes driving a car the week before. He sighed as he decided that he would have to cultivate Joan. At least, there was no personal risk involved. She was as uninterested in him as he was in her. She had made that clear at the outset. "Play along," she had advised him.

Obviously, she wanted a cover for her own activities. He remembered her words on the telephone, "Please—please—please." To whom had she been appealing so desperately? Which of the men who had come to dinner: Glen Forbes, Charlie Forbes, Paul Brooks, Jerome Cook? On the surface, either of the Forbes men would be more likely. They were young and they both had exceptional charm. But Joan had made that malicious comment about seeing Forbes drive a car. If she were interested in the man she would scarcely be stirring up suspicion against him unless— unless, he conceded reluctantly, she was trying a little blackmail to achieve her own ends.

Paul Brooks, Blair Masters had declared, had a roving eye. Was Joan interested in him? He appeared to be Forbes' only ostensible enemy and the one person who had profited by either of the murders. But if he had killed his niece, would he take the needless chance of stirring up rumors? Wouldn't he, for his own protection, be thankful to let sleeping dogs lie? And why kill the second woman? Why, above all, kill her in the same way?

Of course, if Brooks could discredit the Center and build his housing project he would make a great deal of money. Tonight he had deliberately baited Miss Kenyon, or prompted her, into making clear that she had come to Bridgetown to collect material on murder. Ten days earlier, Forbes had not known, or had said he did not know, who was behind the rumors. Then why had Brooks suddenly come out in the open?

Mr. Potter got up to pace the floor, dissatisfied with the trend his thoughts were taking. He had an uncomfortable feeling that the whole contentious dinner party had been cleverly staged, that he had watched the puppets and failed to see the strings. For one thing was clear, whatever Brooks' position might be, he had not been driving the car which so nearly struck Blair Masters.

Which of the Forbes men had been at the wheel? In the excitement of the moment no one had noticed from which side of the car they had come running. Charlie was accident prone. Everyone said that. If it had not been for the two deaths, the incident might easily be dismissed as sheer accident. And yet, accident or not, if he had not been standing by, Blair Masters would have been run over.

Thinking of Blair Masters, Mr. Potter frowned. When he had first talked to her, a plan had leaped into his mind. He had intended to use her as live bait for a trap. The one possibility he had failed to take into account was that Blair might become personally involved with Forbes. But tonight, seeing the hot color rise in her face, he had known that, whether she was aware of it or not, she was attracted to the man, which meant that her instinct for survival would be dulled. For a heart-wrenching moment Mr. Potter recalled how completely it can be dulled and then, with the self-discipline he had learned so painfully, he pulled his mind back to the immediate problem.

I'll keep an eye on her, he decided. If necessary, I'll get someone to help me guard her, because the damnable feature of this affair is that it is not finished. Something is going to happen. The whole atmosphere of the dinner party tonight made that obvious.

Early in the morning he was out of doors before the Brennings had come downstairs. He went to study the tire marks in the parking area. The only conclusion he arrived at was that, if the driver had been excited and overwrought, as Charlie Forbes had seemed to be, it could have been an accident. One more coincidence in the chain of coincidences that had strained Kurt Tyson's credulity to the breaking point.

The Brennings were at breakfast when he came in to help himself at the sideboard where hot dishes were set out, buffet style. When he had seated himself he apologized to his hostess for his responsibility in suggesting that Miss Kenyon come to dinner.

She waved aside his apology. "No one would dream of blaming you for it, Hiram. I've always heard that writers are peculiar people. But I've just been telling Stanley that something has to be done. That woman obviously intends to write a book about Glen and she'll have to be stopped. Glen ought to sue her. Or rather Stanley ought to do it. After all, he handles Glen's affairs for him. I hope I never live through such an evening again! What with Paul being as disagreeable as possible—"

"Then why," Brenning put in irritably, "did you ask him to dinner when the Forbes men were coming? You should have known there would be trouble. Lately Brooks never misses a chance to be offensive to Glen."

"Well, Joan wanted him. She simply insisted." His wife's voice trailed off.

Brenning gave her a quick, troubled look and then turned to his guest. "Did you manage Miss Kenyon all right?"

"Oh, yes. I just dumped the woman on her bed to sleep it off. Ever hear of her before?" he added casually.

"I haven't time for books. *Life* and *Newsweek* are about all I read, and *The New York Times*. Naturally. That was a close shave Miss Masters had."

"Very close," Mr. Potter agreed grimly.

"I've been thinking it over. It simply must have been Charlie at the wheel," Mrs. Brenning declared. "After all, Glen won't even ride as a passenger if he can avoid it. That's one reason why he closed up his house and arranged living quarters at the Center. And Charlie simply should not be allowed to drive at all!"

She broke off as a thickset maid with a broad flat face like a tablespoon spoke quietly to her. She went out of the room and returned a few minutes later.

"That was Charlie Forbes," she announced, "telephoning to apologize for his behavior last night."

"Did he say anything about nearly running down Miss Masters?" her husband asked.

"He said he didn't remember it. But Glen had told him what he had done."

"That settles it, Beulah," Brenning said in a tone of decision. "Charlie Forbes has come to this house for the last time."

"Heaven knows I hope so," his wife said fervently, "but Joan—"

"We have spoiled our girl but this time there is to be no appeal. Joan must accept our decision."

Joan laughed from the doorway. "Look who is being the heavy father!" She came in to kiss the top of Brenning's head and wave to Mr. Potter before going to the sideboard. This morning she was bright eyed, glowing, tingling with an excitement that made itself felt like an electric charge. "What decision must I accept?"

Her father gave her a wary glance. "Charlie Forbes has been here for the last time."

Joan's eyes flickered. She forked up scrambled eggs and bacon and brought her plate to the table. "Of course, Charlie was higher than a kite. But then so was that poisonous woman Hiram dragged in." She giggled. "The man who butchers women! What a bombshell. I wouldn't have missed it for anything on earth. Hiram, darling, you know the most fascinating people."

Mr. Potter accepted her baiting amiably but he wondered what the girl was up to, aware of a jubilation, a kind of triumph that she scarcely attempted to conceal. Mrs. Brenning, too, was watching her daughter uneasily.

"And what are you two young people planning to do with yourselves this morning?" she asked.

"I'm so sorry, Hiram," Joan said, her eyes fever bright, "I've got to go to New York for a day's shopping. But I'll be back tomorrow and we'll plan something then. Today," she grinned maliciously, "you can cultivate the lovely Miss Masters."

"But, Joan—" Mrs. Brenning expostulated.

"New York?" Mr. Potter interjected smoothly. "Fine! I have to run down myself. See my broker. I'll give you a lift."

The fear faded from Mrs. Brenning's face. Joan was taken aback. Mr. Potter was aware in some amusement of a quick change of plans.

"Wonderful," she said. "I'll be ready in an hour. I've got to do some telephoning first."

"Where do you stay in New York?"

"At the Plaza," Mrs. Brenning answered. "Such a nice hotel. I always feel Joan will be safe there."

Mr. Potter collected a shaving kit. Then, with fifty minutes to spare, he drove down to the Center. A trail of smoke from the chimney led him to the salt box.

In a few moments he followed Forbes upstairs to his small living room. He accepted Blair's presence, drinking coffee before the open fire, without comment. Forbes explained that after the night before he had not expected her to come. In fact, he had assumed that no one would show up at the Center that day and he had been lounging around with a second cup of coffee when she had made a most welcome appearance.

Mr. Potter took up Forbes' last remark but one. He hadn't expected anyone to show up? But wasn't there an employee of some sort, a bookkeeper?

There was a bookkeeper, Forbes agreed, but he had telephoned early to say he wouldn't be in. He had a cold. Probably cold feet. Harrison had been caught in defalcation and, Forbes said grimly, he intended to prosecute.

"Ordinarily, I'd let it go because, after all, he was Evelyn's cousin. But he threatened me. He seemed to think I'd be afraid to prosecute, so I've got to do it." He added without anger, "The damned fool is bringing it on himself. But at least this is something that has to come out in the open. I've had a bellyful of rumors."

"Why did he think you'd be afraid to prosecute?"

Forbes frowned. "Damned if I know. George was always a nasty piece of work but he seems to think because I hired him I'm an easy mark."

Mr. Potter turned to Blair. "I'm driving Joan Brenning to New York this morning and I won't be back until sometime tomorrow. I just wanted to make sure you're all right."

"Quite all right," she declared.

"How is Miss Kenyon this morning?"

"Still asleep when I left the house, thank heaven!" Blair described the interlude in the night. "And you were right, Mr. Potter. The woman is afraid. Oh, and I found out something about her. She comes from a small town in New York. Elmwood."

Forbes looked from one to the other. "I'd been under the impression," he said, "that Miss Masters was to be my assistant but she appears to be yours. I take it you've explained the situation to her."

Mr. Potter looked at the vein pulsing in Forbes' temple, at Blair's startled eyes, and said peacefully, "We owed her an explanation. I think you'll acknowledge that. And before you go off the deep end, I might say that last night I offered to take her back to New York and pay for her summer. Miss Masters refused to go because of the effect her sudden departure would have on public opinion here in town in regard to you. And it was her own suggestion, not mine, to see what she could really find out about the enigmatic Miss Kenyon."

Forbes was at a loss. "Sorry," he said. "I—that's very kind of you." He looked at Blair intently for a moment but he did not seem to see her. "Stanley Brenning telephoned a few moments ago. He wants to threaten the Kenyon woman with a law suit if she goes ahead with her book."

"How do you feel about it?" Mr. Potter asked curiously.

"I haven't much choice, have I?" Forbes laughed harshly. "If I don't sue her I look guilty. You'd better work fast, Potter. This situation is rapidly getting out of control. And on top of everything else, Miss Masters was nearly killed last night."

"Which one of you was driving?" Mr. Potter asked.

Again the pulse beat in Forbes' temple. "I—do—not—drive—a—car. And Joan was mistaken in thinking she ever saw me do so."

"Is there any reason you know of why Joan should be a hostile witness?"

Forbes seemed to be genuinely surprised. "Good lord, no. It was a pure mistake on her part."

"Maybe. Leaving chivalry and all that aside for the moment, is there any emotional bond between Joan and your cousin Charlie?"

Coffee splashed into the saucer as Forbes set down his cup. "I don't know anything about Charlie's love affairs," he said.

He started to light a cigarette, saw that his hand was

shaking and tossed the cigarette into the fire.

"I'd like to make some telephone calls, if I may," Mr. Potter said.

"Downstairs in my office. Help yourself."

Mr. Potter nodded and went out. There was silence in the living room for a moment. Blair, aware of Forbes' intent eyes on her face, stirred uneasily.

"As soon as he has made his calls," she said at length, finding it necessary to break the silence, "I'll get to work."

Forbes stood leaning against the mantel looking down at her. "Miss Masters, I had hoped it would not be necessary to discuss the situation here but now we can't escape it. I gather that you know a lot of people believe I am a murderer twice over."

Blair nodded without looking up.

"There's one point we've got to get straight," he said sharply. "Are you afraid of me?"

This time her eyes came up to his face. "No," she said. She added breathlessly, "Of course not."

"Well, that's that. I had to be sure."

The front door banged open, Charlie Forbes spoke to Mr. Potter, ran up the stairs and came into the room. Again, looking from one man to the other, Blair felt that she was seeing the two sides of a coin.

"Good morning, Miss Masters. I met Potter downstairs, telephoning. He said I'd find you up here." For a moment his eyes rested on the two coffee cups. "I called the Brennings and groveled but I wanted to make my apology to you in person. Glen tells me I nearly ran you down last night. The truth is that I must have blacked out. I don't remember even driving the car. But if Glen says I did, I must have. Will you try to forgive me? If I promise to be on my best behavior?" He gave her a beguiling grin.

Blair found herself smiling at him and took the hand he held out to her.

"Prove that you mean it," he begged. "Have dinner with me tomorrow, will you, and we'll take in a movie. Wish I could make it tonight but—I'm tied up. Say yes! Please say yes. Otherwise I'll think you don't trust me."

Blair was aware of the tension between the two men, though Forbes had not moved and Charlie had not looked in his direction. She had an impression that Charlie was speaking to his cousin rather than to her. It was annoying to be put in this awkward position between the two men but there was, after all, no excuse for refusing Charlie's invitation.

"Thank you," she said at last, "that will be fun."

"You are an angel. All a man needs," Charlie declared oratorically, "is the faith of a good woman. I'll pick you up tomorrow about six. Okay?" He went on quickly, ran down the stairs and Blair heard him start his car and move away with a clash of gears.

Forbes had not moved from his position beside the mantel. His face was expressionless but the vein throbbed again in his temple. Blair longed to say, "I don't want to go out with Charlie but I didn't know how to avoid it.

Mr. Potter came up the stairs and looked thoughtfully from one silent person to the other.

"Make your calls?" Forbes asked.

"Yes, thanks. Everything is under control. I'll be off now." He turned to Blair. "What was that town the Kenyon woman came from? Elmwood? Right. I'll be back tomorrow." He added soberly, "Until then, be careful."

When he had gone Forbes pulled the screen in front of the fire. "When you're ready," he said, and Blair got up without a word. From the window she caught sight of Mr. Potter hurrying across the miniature green toward his convertible. He looked at his watch, his lips moving.

She smiled. "He's rather like the white rabbit, isn't he?"

Forbes' mind seemed to come back from a long way. "Potter? You couldn't be more mistaken. He is one hell of a guy. Never stampeded into anything. I met a commanding officer of his once who told me how he stood up under punishment. It isn't the big guy who flexes his muscles and roars the loudest who has the real strength. On the whole, I'd rather have Potter on my side than any other man I know."

He was thoughtful for a moment. "And I'd hate to have him against me. He could be dangerous. Very dangerous."

9

That feverish excitement still burned high when Joan got into the convertible beside Mr. Potter.

"What a car!" she exclaimed. "Will you let it out, really let it out?"

"Not now," Mr. Potter said as he eased it through the covered bridge and made a sharp left turn onto the highway.

Joan shivered. "I'm always glad to get out of that place alive. It frightens me, makes me feel trapped. And after what happened there, I don't see why someone doesn't burn it down. I hate covered bridges anyhow. All these hangovers from the past. That's what gets me about Glen Forbes. Such an exciting looking man but he is always trying to turn back the clock. Instead of letting some life get into this dead town he wants to collect all the rubbish our ancestors had sense enough to relegate to the attic."

Mr. Potter, his hands quiet on the wheel, remarked, "You sound like Paul Brooks."

She shot him a quick glance. Then she shrugged. "Well, at least he makes sense. And it isn't as though Glen owed the community anything. What have they done for him, I'd like to know. It's just plain ridiculous to see a rich man like that live in a couple of makeshift rooms up over an office, though I don't blame him much for wanting to get out of his house. It must have been full of ghosts. Poor guy! But he could have built a new house with no memories in it."

"Someone would see that the memories were kept alive," Mr. Potter suggested.

"I guess so." Joan shrugged off the thought. "Personally, when I marry I intend to have a Frank Lloyd Wright house and all modern furniture."

"I take it you intend to marry money."

Joan laughed excitedly. "That can be arranged." She fell silent for a little while and then, unable to contain her bottled-up excitement, she began to fidget. "Which of these dinkuses turns on the radio?"

"None of them," Mr. Potter said firmly. He had no intention of driving over a hundred miles accompanied by soap operas and singing commercials. His foot pressed on the pedal and the car leaped forward.

Joan watched the speedometer, entranced. "Glory!" she whispered, "I've never ridden this fast before."

Having succeeded in distracting her attention, Mr. Potter imperceptibly began to reduce speed.

"It's so terribly exciting to drive like this," Joan said. "I couldn't live without a car. Glen is really a dope not to have one."

"I thought you said he did have one."

"Well, I didn't actually see him myself. Someone who was driving with me thought it was Glen. Of course, he and Charlie look so much alike—but if it had been Charlie, he'd have said so, wouldn't he?"

Mr. Potter made no comment.

"Unless he was mad at Glen. Glen really rides him too hard. No one is ever going to tell me what to do, even for all the dough Glen hands out to Charlie. Take it all in all, Charlie earns it."

"Did you know either of Forbes' wives?"

"Both of them," Joan said, "and why a fascinating man like that got stuck the way he did, baffles me. Though I'll have to admit that Connie was good looking and a lot of fun."

"I remember her. Forbes used to bring her up to college for the dances. She was very popular."

"Very," Joan said, her voice freighted with meaning.

Mr. Potter let the car slow down, risked a glance at her face. "And what is that supposed to mean?"

"Well," Joan said, obviously enjoying herself, "it

was one of those marriages. Connie was the girl next door and the Brooks and Forbes parents brought them together. Oh, they were fond of each other but there was no big love affair. More habit and propinquity than anything else. And, at least, Connie was attractive; she could entertain Glen's friends, and all that. But when it came to that drip, Evelyn Harrison—"

"What was she like?"

"Like a kitten that's been left out in the rain," Joan declared, "plain and dull and sort of pathetic. The kind you see waiting on customers in bargain basements. She usually had a cold and a red nose. Emily Cook says Glen was sorry for her, and I must say she acted as though she was crazy about him, but personally I don't see how anyone could give either of them house room."

"Either of whom?"

"The Harrisons. Evelyn and her cousin George. And what a wet smack he is! I've always thought they fastened themselves on Glen like barnacles."

"Somehow," Mr. Potter remarked, "Forbes doesn't strike me as being the sort of man to accept that kind of thing passively. He's quite a lot of man."

"I suppose," Joan insinuated, "it would depend on the circumstances."

"His two wives don't seem to have had much in common," Mr. Potter said idly.

Joan giggled. "Oh, yes, they did!"

"What was that? Come on, you know you're dying to tell me."

"Charlie Forbes."

"That," Mr. Potter admitted, "is an item of local gossip I hadn't picked up. If it's any satisfaction to you, you have completely floored me."

"Actually," Joan said, "Connie was the one who did the chasing. She always had to be going somewhere and if Glen was busy she would get Charlie to take her. A lot of people talked about it because Connie started fooling around with him as soon as she got back from her honeymoon. Glen never said a word, but you never

know what Glen's thinking. As for Evelyn, Dad saw
Charlie coming out of the Forbes house late one night
when he knew for a fact that Glen had gone to Boston.
So—" she leaned forward to switch on the radio and
this time Mr. Potter made no protest.

Was that what Forbes had been holding back, the
fact that his cousin had been involved with both his
wives? Was that what he wanted Mr. Potter to discover
for himself, what he could not bring himself to reveal?
Was that at the root of the tension between him and
his cousin? Mr. Potter recalled Charlie's evident interest in Blair, the accident, and for a moment battled an
almost overwhelming temptation to make a U turn and
send the convertible rocketing back to Bridgetown.

One job at a time, he reminded himself. Blair will be
safe until I get back. Bound to be. Meanwhile, there is
Joan and the man she is going to New York to meet.
Which of the four men is it and what is she up to?

As the high buildings began to loom into sight Joan
gave an ecstatic sigh.

"Like it, don't you?" he said.

"Mad about it. New York has everything. Excitement—"

"Don't you ever get tired of excitement?"

"When I do I'll be half dead."

He came down the ramp at Fifty-seventh street and
worked his way east. On Fifth Avenue he turned north
to the Plaza. While Joan's suitcase and cosmetic bag
were taken out of the car, he looked around. A schol-
arly appearing man with a round face, round spectacles
and a briefcase, who had been watching the pigeons,
glanced at him, turned for a look at Joan and then
drifted into the lobby. Mr. Potter arranged to pick her
up at eight the next morning and drove off. He had
done all he could.

Before the Gramercy Park house he pulled the convertible in at the curb and locked it. Tito Petrella who,
with his wife Antonia, had worked for his mother, was
standing in the areaway. As usual when he was not po-
liced—Tito was unshaven and without the trim white

© Lorillard 1975

C'mon

Come for the filter. You'll stay for the taste.

KING SIZE

KENT
WITH
THE FAMOUS MICRONITE FILTER

KING SIZE

KENT
WITH
THE FAMOUS MICRONITE FILTER

Newport

Alive with pleasure!

Newport
20
CLASS A
CIGARETTES

Newport®

MENTHOL KINGS

7 mg. "tar", 1.2 mg. nicotine, av. per cigarette, FTC Report Apr. '75.

Warning: The Surgeon General Has Determined
That Cigarette Smoking Is Dangerous to Your Health.

jacket that was provided for him. As he caught sight of his employer he darted back for his jacket and returned, fingering his stubbly chin sheepishly.

Mr. Potter shook his head. "What am I going to do with you, Tito?"

Tito flung out his arms. "I didn't expect you for another half hour."

Mr. Potter laughed and started up the front steps. Tito called after him, "The young lady has already come. She's waiting in the drawing room."

The front door opened onto a hallway with a beautiful curving stairway, a black and white tesselated floor, a long Florentine mirror. Antonia bustled out of the kitchen, the faint mustache on her upper lip dewy with her exertions, heavy breasts seeming to thrust themselves through the fabric of her dress, a phenomenon which always filled Mr. Potter with a faint alarm.

She beamed. "I'll have lunch ready in fifteen minutes. The young lady is here." She did not attempt to conceal her delight.

The Petrellas, as Mr. Potter was amusedly aware, had many differences but on one point they were as one. Both of them believed that what Mr. Potter needed was a love affair, and the girl waiting now in the drawing room was their choice, had been their choice ever since they had seen pictures of her spread across the newspapers, revealing her undraped charms as a model.

Mr. Potter opened the drawing room door and went in smiling. "Hello, Opal."

Opal Reed ran to meet him with a flurry of skirts and planted a moist but enthusiastic kiss on his chin. She was about twenty with a spectacular figure, steady brown eyes and a warm, generous mouth.

"Hiram!" She hugged him and then slipped off her shoes and curled up in a chair. "Did you see Sam? What's it all about? We're so excited we can hardly bear it."

He smiled at her with affectionate amusement. She was really unusually attractive. With a figure like that she could cause a stampede but what really won one's heart was her sheer delight in living. Opal's capacity for boundless happiness, her fresh and inexhaustible interest in her world made Joan Brenning's feverish need for excitement seem pallid.

"I saw Sam," he assured her. "He was waiting outside the Plaza as we drove up. I can't tell you how much I appreciate the way you both dropped everything to give me a hand."

"Baloney," Opal scoffed. "In the first place, we knew it would be fun."

His eyebrows shot up. "Fun?"

"Well, interesting, anyhow. It's queer about you, Hiram, the way things happen where you are."

He stirred uneasily and she gave him an anxious look. "It isn't anything bad, is it?"

"I hope not."

"Look, Hiram, there won't be anyone killed, the way it was before?"

"Someone has already been killed," he said quietly, "but it was a long time ago and there won't be any more." For an uncomfortable moment he remembered the fleeting panic he had experienced on the trip down to New York. Something about Blair Masters and Charlie Forbes. Then he dismissed it firmly from his mind.

"At any rate," he told her, "there's nothing for you to worry about. You and Sam won't be involved this time."

Opal was outraged. "I wasn't worrying about that. You know darned well if you asked for my right arm or Sam's you could have it. When I think what we owe you—no, I've got to tell you and there's no use looking miserable, the way you do every time I try to thank you. You know how Sam was. Nothing more or less than a con man. He didn't even want to settle down. And then after that mess last year he began to see there wasn't any sense in living outside the law. That it was lonely, like you said."

"He was bound to find that out for himself in time."

"Maybe," she said skeptically. "Anyhow, he's making good on his job because he can ferret out crooks. You were smart, Hiram, when you got him work as an insurance investigator. He likes it. And he likes carrying real business papers in that briefcase instead of an extra shirt in case he has to run away. And he doesn't even wipe off his fingerprints from glasses when he's in a restaurant. Hardly ever." She added proudly, "You've never seen a more respectable man."

Mr. Potter watched the triumphant face affectionately. "And how about you? Last I heard, you were being talked about as a promising starlet."

"Oh, that," she said with exaggerated indifference. "There was nothing in that."

Mr. Potter tipped his fair head a little to one side as he studied her. "Come on now, what happened? You've got a figure that would make Marilyn Monroe swoon with envy. You are far from hideous when the eyes finally reach your face. And don't try to tell me that you aren't photogenic. So?"

"Well," Opal said, "I ran into a wolf pack out there in Hollywood. Every date ended in a wrestling match. I can't really act, you know, I'm just nice to look at. But no one was satisfied just to look. Anyhow, Sam wasn't there. So I came back and got a job modeling in an exclusive shop."

"And?" he prodded.

She flushed but the candid brown eyes met his levelly. "And I'm waiting until he gets around to noticing me."

Mr. Potter laughed. "Why don't you give him up as a bad job and try someone else?"

She shook her head and though she joined in his laugh her eyes were serious. "Just a one-man woman, that's me," she mourned. "But I'll get him yet and I'll make him like it. Now tell me what this is all about and why you want Sam to shadow that girl and what you expect me to do."

Tito, shaved and contrite, came in to say there was a telephone call from Mr. Trumble. Mr. Potter left the double doors open between the drawing room and library while he answered, so that Opal could hear the conversation.

"Hello, Sam! . . . She what? . . . yes, keep after her. All I want is to know who the man is."

He turned to Opal who was hovering at his shoulder. "Well," he said slowly, "well, well."

Tito announced lunch and he led Opal through the library and into the dining room which ran across the back of the narrow house and looked out onto a pocket handkerchief of a garden with a small fountain. Opal had come a long way. She was no longer self-conscious nor awkward. She let him seat her and then leaned across the table. "What's wrong?"

He told her the story of Glen Forbes from the beginning to the point where he had left Joan Brenning at the Plaza and Sam Trumble had taken up his watch.

"What did Sam say?"

"Joan didn't register at the hotel. She made a long telephone call from the lobby and ate a quick lunch. Now she is having her bags taken out to a taxi."

"Well?"

"I hope so. Only for some reason I'm anxious about her. Joan is a born fool and she is infatuated with one of those four men."

"But what of it? I mean, what does it have to do with the Forbes fellow and his wives?"

"I don't know," Mr. Potter admitted. "I just have a hunch about it. All four of those men are tied pretty closely together, in one way and another, and Joan—there's something odd about her. And she has deliberately lied to me over and over. There must be a reason for it. I'm uneasy."

"You think she's in danger, don't you?"

"She could be. There's some man at Bridgetown whom it isn't healthy for women to know. Now eat your lunch and tell me about modeling. We can't do anything more now. Sam won't let her get into any real trouble."

"At least," Opal said, "she can't be meeting your friend, this Glen Forbes. He's still in Bridgetown. And that's the main thing, isn't it?"

"It helps," Mr. Potter admitted.

10

The taxi driver stopped for a light.

"Don't get too far behind," Sam Trumble warned him. "I don't want to lose her."

"Get wise, brother," the driver told him. "When you have to shadow them you've already lost them."

"Not me," Sam said firmly. "I'm not married, thank God!"

"Detective?"

"In a way. Actually, I'm doing this for a friend."

"The poor jerk," the driver remarked. "The way I look at it is, if the guy can't keep her he'd be better off to let her go. Hell, you can't watch a woman all the time. And there are always plenty more. Believe me, I see enough of them in this racket. Worked the midnight to eight o'clock shift for five months. After that, nothing would surprise me."

The driver threaded his way through traffic and Sam watched the taxi ahead. Through the back window he could see the girl's blond hair and the scrap of red medallions and veiling that passed for a hat. Where could she be going? They were already on the outskirts of New York and still moving steadily north.

"He's turning in," the driver said sharply, and slid into the right-hand lane. He pulled off the highway and stopped the car.

"What's up?" Sam asked.

"I can follow her if you like but I thought you didn't want the girl to know she was being shadowed."

Sam looked at the long trim-looking motel. "Oh, I see."

"Getting out here?"

"We'll wait until we see what she does. She may be meeting someone and going on."

The taxi ahead had stopped at the office. In a few moments the girl came out, a big tagged key in her hand and signaled the driver who parked in front of Number 15 and carried the girl's luggage inside. Then he came out and drove away.

"All right," Sam decided. "You can leave me here. At least she can't get away."

I hope, he added silently. This he had not figured on, being stuck at a motel without any means of transportation if the girl should leave in a hurry. But it must be all right or Mr. Potter would have made other arrangements. Sam, who was not endowed with an oversupply of faith in his fellowmen, had blind faith in Mr. Potter.

He paid off the driver and, carrying his briefcase, went into the office. The manager was a brisk middle-aged woman who looked him over quickly and liked what she saw. People usually liked Sam Trumble. It was his stock in trade. His face was as guileless as a choir boy's, his manners open and earnest, his smile candid and friendly. Even on people who should have known better he made an impression of somewhat naive honesty.

While he told a rambling story about being picked up in the morning by friends on a motor tour his eyes caught the registration page which was still open. The last entry read: "Mr. & Mrs. Alvin Owen, Baltimore, Maryland."

"You're lucky," the manager said. "Usually people make reservations in advance and we don't often have a vacancy at the last moment. But a guy reserved two rooms for tonight and canceled this morning. Rented one of them just before you came in. Yours is the last."

He left his briefcase in Number 16 and listened for a moment to the sounds the girl made as she unpacked. She was singing to herself. He strolled outside. There was a public telephone next to the office and he closed the door of the booth. When he had made his report to Mr. Potter he returned to his own section, stretched out on the bed and read the *Daily News* from cover to cover. As the afternoon advanced there was more activity around the motel, cars stopping for the night, doors opening and closing. It was a decorous place and, so far as Sam could make out, the clientele was sedate, made up of people who didn't like big city hotels or who were afraid to venture into New York traffic.

As the lights began to fade, he heard the shower run in the next section. The girl was apparently getting ready for her date with "Mr. Owen." Sam looked at his watch. Five-thirty. He couldn't remain holed up here indefinitely. Some time or other he'd have to go out to eat. He had already skipped lunch and Sam was a man who took eating seriously.

He let himself out and went to the office. Yes, the manager told him, there was an excellent restaurant about half a mile up the highway. She recollected that he was without a car. Or there was a hamburger stand a block to the east. Clean and good but not fancy.

Sam decided to take a chance. The girl wouldn't leave. She had a good hide-out for the night and tomorrow morning she would be back in the lobby of the Plaza, waiting for Mr. Potter, all girlish innocence. He walked to the hamburger stand, ate a hearty meal with undiscriminating enthusiasm, and returned to the motel. There was still no car outside Number 15. Inside his own section he put his ear to the wall. Not a sound. Nothing. The place was empty. His bird had flown.

For the next hour and a half Sam lived in an agony of self-reproach. What would Potter think of him? What would Opal think? Opal who believed he was competent to deal with any emergency. Curious how much he minded having her know that he had been a fool, that he had been tricked by a mere kid. Curious how sure he was that even when she knew it she would be quick to defend him, to find excuses for him.

When the car door slammed at seven-thirty he was

so deep in anathematizing himself that he barely noticed it. Then a key grated in a lock, so close that it seemed to be in his own room, there were footsteps and voices next door. The girl had come back and this time with "Mr. Owen." He realized then that they had merely gone out to dinner and mopped his head in relief.

After a few moments he let himself out quietly, leaving his door on the latch. In front of Number 15 stood a shabby Mercury with a Maryland license plate. He jotted down the number and went around to the back of the motel, counting windows until he came to Number 15. Lights burned behind tightly closed Venetian blinds. The window had been raised a few inches. He pressed his ear against it as the lights went out.

Time passed. Sam's round eyes grew rounder. His lips pursed in a silent whistle. At length he went back to his own section and undressed. He might as well get some sleep while he could. The couple next door wouldn't leave until morning. The night before, he had slept only four hours. Most of the time he had sat in on a poker game with a man whom he had encouraged to win and who had talked trustingly of how he had burned down his factory for the insurance. It had been a good night's work, particularly as the other man in the game had obligingly agreed to serve as a witness. But Sam had to sleep some time.

Sam slept.

What awakened him was the sound of a door closing. Even before he was wide awake he had leaped out of bed, run to open the Venetian blinds and look out. The girl was getting into the Mercury with the Maryland license plate. The man whom he was to identify for Mr. Potter was already at the wheel. As the car had been backed in, Sam could not see his face, could see nothing but a gray felt hat and gray overcoat. He jerked on his trousers, ran to the door and opened it. The motor roared and the car pulled away from the motel, weaved its way into the highway traffiic and disappeared.

II

"A librarian?" Opal repeated dubiously.

"A librarian," Mr. Potter insisted. "As a model, even as a Hollywood starlet, you wouldn't strike the right note. Miss Kenyon is a writer. She must have spent hours in the local library. They'd know about her."

"And how long do you think it would take them to know about me?" Opal pointed out. "I don't know a thing about libraries. And then I'm just not the type."

Opal was reasonableness itself. For her to persist in her stubbornness meant that the situation was serious. Mr. Potter surveyed her critically. Even in the correct "little black dress" so dearly loved by couturiers, her body was undeniably spectacular. Nor was this the face that launched a thousand books. His own face fell, a reaction not typical in men who looked at Opal.

"You see?" she demanded mournfully.

"I see."

They both sighed.

"Look," she said, "I know what. I'll be a newspaper reporter. Sometimes they take girls with sex appeal." She shared Mr. Potter's depression. "Because there's no getting around it, I have sex appeal."

Unexpectedly he laughed. "Thank God for that!" he declared fervently. "Well, let's say you are a reporter. Think you can manage?"

Opal's self-confidence and optimism returned. "You wait and see. I'll be back with the dope before you know it."

When she got off the bus in Elmwood, Opal was directed to the library. She was also followed by whistles which outwardly she ignored but inwardly found reassuring. It was all right for women to disapprove of whistles but when the day came for Opal to walk out, whistleless—

Inside the library there were dim lights and the same musty smells. In front of her was the checking desk. At the left a long room with a narrow table strewn with periodicals. Chairs had been drawn up as though it were a conference table and some dozen women were sitting around it, talking in a low sibilant murmur.

Opal, who had anticipated finding the librarian alone, was taken aback. This was no atmosphere for confidences. As she stood hesitating, the woman behind the desk looked up and nodded toward the periodical room.

"Civil Defense in there," she said and went back to making out cards.

You see, Opal mentally addressed Mr. Potter, she didn't think for a moment that I wanted a book.

She turned toward the group of women. Perhaps she could sit in the background, unnoticed, until the meeting broke up. If it didn't last too long she would still be able to manage a confidential talk with the librarian before the place closed for the night. But Opal was not one to pass, unnoticed, even in a feminine group.

A stout elderly woman came up and shook hands. "I am Mrs. Williams," she said, "and delighted to have such a fine turnout. I don't believe—?"

"I am Opal Reed. Sorry I forgot my press card."

Mrs. Williams beamed. "Girls," she called, and rapped on the table for order, "girls, we have a newspaper reporter with us to do a story on what Elmwood is accomplishing for Civil Defense. Do sit down, Miss Reed. We're delighted to have you with us."

Opal did not know what a reporter was supposed to do but she pulled out the notebook and pencils with which Mr. Potter had thoughtfully supplied her. Mrs. Williams made clear that the first thing expected of her was to make a list of those present, being careful to see that all the names were correctly spelled. There were scattered suggestions that their husbands' positions might be mentioned, or the fact that Mrs. Fisk's daughter Cora was to be married in June, just a quiet home wedding, but Mrs. Williams proved her leadership by tactfully disposing of them.

While the ladies of the Civil Defense got down to

business, Opal looked on with the whole-hearted interest that made living so tirelessly fascinating to her. Never having heard of Elmwood until three hours earlier, she was naturally amazed to discover that it was regarded as a danger point of great strategic importance. If.The Bomb were dropped anywhere on American soil, it was apt to be directed at Elmwood.

While the meeting progressed, Opal was awed to observe that the ladies were directing their remarks less to one another than to her. One woman in particular, a tense woman with a fretful voice, who was snubbed by the others, directed a perfect barrage of dire statistics at the girl's defenseless head.

A Calamity Jane, Opal decided. She knows what happens to everyone in town, expects the worst, and wears herself out for causes that would get along better without her. The kind of woman who screams "Fire" in a theater.

"I realize," the woman raised her voice determinedly over the chairwoman's efforts to shut her off, "that it is unpleasant to hear these facts. But we cannot evade them. We should not evade them. We must anticipate the worst because, in my experience, the worst is what happens."

Opal, who took a natural pleasure in being proved right in her judgment, beamed her delight. Which was a tactical error as it immediately suggested to Calamity Jane that her words were about to be immortalized, or at least set into cold type for all the world to read.

"Miss Reed, who has probably studied the whole field of Civil Defense in much broader aspects than we can expect to do here in Elmwood, will agree with me, I know."

Opal blinked in astonishment at this tribute to her omniscience and managed to scrawl some wiggly lines in the hope that they would pass for shorthand.

"Of course," Calamity Jane rushed on, still addressing Opal, while the other members of the committee glared helplessly, "we know that Elmwood is only a small town, with all the small town's drawbacks, but it is up to date, too. We have a simply foolproof scheme for evacuating New York City to Elmwood in case of a bombing attack."

"Wouldn't it," Opal suggested timidly, "be rather crowded?"

"Oh, that," Calamity Jane dismissed the problem airily. "When the time comes we'll find a way. The impossible just takes a little longer."

"Mrs. Ferguson," the chairwoman said in desperation, "is something of a local historian, Miss Reed. I'm sure she'd be delighted to tell you about our town. After the meeting." The last three words were spoken with such firmness that Calamity Jane subsided and the rest of the committee continued their discussion in peace.

When they had adjourned, Mrs. Williams came to shake hands with Opal and assure herself that the reporter had all the material she required.

"And now," she concluded, "perhaps you will come home with me for a cup of tea or," she laughed coyly, "a little cocktail."

Opal thanked her. She had to get back at once to—what had Mr. Potter told her?—to file her story. She turned to find the tenacious Mrs. Ferguson at her side. Mrs. Williams, knowing when she was outmaneuvered, graciously took leave.

Calamity Jane eagerly drew a chair close to Opal's and began to relate the history of Elmwood from its founding, with digressions to point out her own peculiar fitness for the work of local historian.

Opal found her attention wandering but brought it back manfully. If anyone could tell her what Mr. Potter wanted to know, Mrs. Ferguson was the woman.

"Yes, Elmwood is really a live wire. Law-abiding. Conscious of its civic responsibilities, though you must not judge us by those incompetent women today. A good town to live in. Practically no crime." Her voice dropped. "At any rate, no sex crimes. And only one murder in twenty years. In fact, we're so law-abiding I always say we wouldn't know what to do if we had a real crime."

"Then what did you do when you had your murder?" Opal asked, looking rapt as she remembered Mr. Potter's instructions.

"Oh, that was twenty years ago. I was just a girl then. And no mystery to it at all. A man killed his wife, strangled her. The daughter saw it happen and called the police."

"How awful for her, having to testify against her own father."

"Yes, it was. It did something to her; she was never the same again. Seemed to think all men were her natural enemies. Once she had a date for a high-school dance and the boy who took her kissed her and she simply clawed him up. Nearly blinded him. After that, she never had another date."

"Whatever became of the poor thing?" Opal asked.

"She stayed on in Elmwood until a few years ago and started writing books about men who killed their wives. I got one at the library once but I couldn't finish it. I had nightmares for weeks. I'd find myself looking at my husband, wondering—" Mrs. Ferguson laughed. "It sounds crazy but then Ann Kenyon was a crazy sort of girl. I'm glad she has gone away."

When she had learned all that Mrs. Ferguson knew, Opal went to the newspaper office and searched the old files. Ann Kenyon had been twelve when her father murdered her mother. The child had been awakened in the night by the sound of her parents quarreling and the murder had been committed before her horrified eyes. She had run out of the house in her nightgown, screaming for help. Her testimony had sent her father to the electric chair.

Opal made a long-distance call to Mr. Potter.

"So that's it," he said after a long silence. "I suppose it could be worse but I don't quite see how. You didn't find out why she went to Bridgetown, did you?"

"She left here four years ago and no one seems to

know what happened to her. She hadn't any close friends in town."

"All right. Thanks a lot. When will you be back?"

"There's a bus in three-quarters of an hour. I'll be back tonight."

"Good girl."

11

In front of the red barn Forbes pulled out a keyring and unlocked the door with its fresh white trim.

"Be careful," he said, "the paint is still wet. Here, you'd better have this." He took a duplicate key off the ring and handed it to her. "This is your domain."

He stepped on a chair and pulled on a light in an unshaded bulb hanging in the middle of the big cavernous room. He looked around doubtfully. The place was a quarter filled with as odd a miscellany as Blair had ever seen. Boxes still unopened. Boxes half unpacked from which spilled hooked rugs. Chairs, tables, desks, chests, mirrors in various stages of disrepair. China dogs and thunder mugs, mustache cups and a broken spinning wheel.

"It doesn't," Forbes admitted, "look so hot. My sister Emily has been picking up stuff here and there but now I examine it there doesn't seem to be much."

The first and most pressing object, Blair thought, was to cheer him up. She did not wonder why this was so important. She knew only that they could not work contentedly together while he was unhappy.

"First," she said briskly and in her most businesslike tone, "I'll make an inventory of what we have on hand. Then we'll need a better light in here and I'll have to have someone lift the heavy things for me so we can get them in some sort of order. Next we'll see whether we can find anyone who knows anything about restoring and refinishing furniture."

Forbes' face brightened. "You don't think the outlook is too hopeless then?"

She forebore looking at the collection of junk. "Not hopeless at all. Of course, we'll have to dig up some more stuff but that's a matter of patience combined with luck."

He prowled around the barn restlessly. The very air of the place seemed to be surcharged with his vitality. Blair found herself wishing that he wasn't quite so overwhelming.

"What I had in mind," he said, "was that there are still people around here who have valuable heirlooms they might want to turn into cash. I wouldn't know an antique from sour apples." He kicked absently at a large coffee grinder. "What's the use of this, for instance?"

Blair laughed. "To some people anything that isn't used any more is valuable. I wouldn't put it past someone to try to turn it into a lamp. They've tried everything else."

"Well, when is an antique an antique and when is it just junk?"

"When someone wants it badly enough to pay for it," Blair said promptly, "it's valuable. Legally, of course, an antique is an object made before 1830. Then it gets into the country duty free. And then it depends on where you live. In New England an antique dates back anywhere from 1850 to colonial times. In the West it may be a Victorian monstrosity belonging to the 1880s."

Forbes grinned at her. "You sound very businesslike when you get on your specialty. Somehow, no one expects so much efficiency from anyone with eyes like yours."

"It isn't efficiency that counts in this business," Blair said, keeping her voice impersonal. "It's a combination of self-confidence plus what Mr. Potter calls 'the patter.'"

His grin faded. "Are you sure you want to go ahead? I don't want you to get involved in any of this—unpleasantness."

"Let's leave it to Mr. Potter," she suggested, "and get on with the job."

"Good. I'll arrange at the bank for a drawing account. There's a lot of good stuff right around Bridgetown. Emily can tell you the most likely places to unearth it. Only—look, we might as well be honest about this. People won't sell to me. They shut the door in my face. They won't have any dealings with me. But they won't feel that way about you. They couldn't possibly feel that way about you. There are," he added, his voice hard, "a number of drawbacks to working with a suspected murderer."

He came back to it like a man pressing on a sore tooth, Blair thought, ignoring his words. She settled on an unopened box. "Suppose you tell me just what you want to make of the Center," she said.

He gave her a cigarette and lighted it. He stood frowning at her. "A kind of clearing house for local talent," he said at length. "A way people can rediscover handicrafts and independence. What Brooks calls 'setting the clock back.' Only there's no choice. The industries have moved out. Unless these people give up their homes and farms and become rootless, chasing after migratory employment—and there's no assurance that they'd find it in the south—they'll have to fall back on themselves. I don't say it's the only answer; I don't even claim that it's the best answer. But I do contend that it is an answer. What do you think?"

"I want to try it," Blair said firmly.

"Even with the local people afraid of me?"

"That won't last."

"You sound awfully sure." He smiled at her. "Why?"

She found that her heart had accelerated its beat. While she groped for an answer he ground his cigarette under foot.

"One thing—I want you to tell me if you encounter the slightest unpleasantness because of working here. At once, do you understand? Now about details. You'll need a station wagon to collect the stuff. You drive, of course."

"Oh, yes."

"Good. Come along with me now. I'll rent a station wagon for you and we'll take care of the drawing account. Then you had better see my sister. She'll tell you where you'll be most likely to find antiques. She knows everyone in a fifty-mile radius and everyone likes Emily. Tomorrow I'll give you a hand in straightening up this place and you'll see what we've got. Sorry I can't be around today but something has come up that I have to attend to. If you're ready—"

When he had locked the barn Blair stood looking around the miniature green. "It's really charming," she declared. "With a couple of months of hard work we could have this place ready for the summer tourist trade."

Forbes stopped for a moment to speak to the foreman in charge of building the Town Hall. Blair was aware that the eyes of the carpenters followed them curiously as Forbes walked beside her along the narrow walk that led out to the highway. They took a muddy worn brick foot path for two blocks to the center of town.

The Bridgetown Bank was on a broad tree-lined avenue. Of the dozen or more stately old homes still standing, at least half of them proved, on closer inspection, to have been converted to business uses. One bore a neat plaque indicating that it was occupied by the Light & Power Company of Bridgetown. One sheltered a gift shop and lending library. One housed Gertrude Fields: Hats. Another had a split personality, one half holding an electric supply shop and the other a bakery. A pseudo-colonial building contained the supermarket. Women in slacks, women in housedresses under coats, women with small children, all carrying big bags of groceries, stopped with a startled look as they saw Forbes walking with a young and pretty stranger.

It was impossible to tell whether Forbes was aware of the speculation in the eyes that watched him. His face was impassive. Blair's cheeks were burning and her eyes were straight ahead as they went up shallow marble steps to the Bridgetown Bank. On the upper floor were dentists, doctors, a real estate agency, a hair dresser and the office of Stanley Brenning.

It was Brenning's unhappy fate inevitably to diminish his own stature by the size of his possessions. Behind an eight-foot mahogany desk, seated in a gigantic brown leather chair, he seemed to slide uncomfortably on a seat that could easily have accommodated two of him. He got up to shake hands with Forbes, to draw a chair closer to the desk for Blair, and to inquire whether she had recuperated from her fright the night before. Avoiding Forbes' eyes, she assured him that she was quite all right.

"That reminds me, Glen," Brenning said. "It's unpleasant and all that, but we're good enough friends to be frank with each other. The thing is, as I told Beulah this morning, we've put up with Charlie too long. Let him get away with murder."

He broke off with a gasp. "I didn't mean that literally, of course," and became aware that he was making the situation worse. Forbes, impassive, silent, made no attempt to help him. "Anyhow, there's no getting away from the fact that he nearly ran down Miss Masters. And his general behavior was offensive. From now on our house is closed to him."

"Not, I hope, on my account," Blair broke in. "He apologized to me this morning. It could have happened to anyone, you know. I should hate, after being here less than a day, to be the cause of disrupting an old friendship."

"You have nothing to do with this, Miss Masters," Brenning assured her. "Don't distress yourself."

Blair glanced uneasily at Forbes, met a frosty look and was silent. Forbes let the awkward silence drag on interminably and then he made no reference either to Charlie or to Blair's defense of him.

"I've come to arrange a drawing account for Miss Masters. She is going to scout around for antiques and she'll need to pay cash for them."

Brenning made notes and said, "I'll take her down now and introduce her to the cashier." The lawyer, however, made no move to get up. "There's one more thing while you're here, Glen. That Kenyon woman stirred up a hell's brew by what she said last night. The story is all over town. I've already heard three separate versions of it myself. They all agree that she came here to do a book about a killer and that you are the protagonist."

"Someone has been busy," Forbes remarked.

"Paul Brooks, of course. It has to be someone who was at the house. Why Beulah asked him—well, anyhow, we can't let that sort of thing go. Can't afford to."

Forbes stretched out his arm and Brenning pushed the telephone toward him. There was a long pause after he had dialed and then Forbes broke the connection. "He doesn't answer. I'll find him later."

Something in his voice made Brenning say in alarm, "Glen, I'll represent you. Don't attempt to handle this yourself. With the Forbes temper—"

"How much," Forbes asked in a flat, repressed voice, "do you expect a man to take?"

"Leave it to me," Brenning insisted. "I was a fool to tell you."

And yet, Blair thought, Stanley Brenning did not appear to be a fool.

II

When she came back to the dealer's from her trial ride in the station wagon, Forbes, who had waited for her, raised his brows. "All right?"

"Wonderful. As easy to handle as a baby carriage. Shall I give you a lift back to the Center?"

"Thanks, I'll walk. I'll see you in the morning, then."

"Wait," she called. "I don't know where your sister lives."

"Go on to the end of the avenue and turn right. Second intersection on the left. There's a white picket fence and the house is set back. Big sprawling white place, looks as though it were built in a series of after thoughts. You can't miss it."

Blair released the brake. In the rearview mirror she saw the dealer standing behind the car, saw his expression.

"Damn them all!" she exploded under her breath. "What's wrong with the people in this town? Hounding an innocent man."

And yet there had been no malice in the man's face. Curiosity, yes; wonder, yes. But most of all there had been fear, fear for her, fear for the woman who had been in Glen Forbes' company.

She eased the car into traffic and followed Forbes' directions. A gravel driveway led up to a side entrance of the white house and for a moment Blair sat staring at it in disbelief. She was roused by the sound of a woman's laugh. Emily Cook, in tailored skirt and twin sweaters, heavy boots on her feet, gloved hand holding a lawn rake, had come across the lawn unnoticed.

"Miss Masters! How nice. Do come in and we'll have lunch. Just the two of us. And don't try to apologize. People of any taste always look that way." She added helplessly, "I don't know what happens to houses, do you? This one started in a perfectly normal way but it got out of control, somehow. I've simply washed my hands of it and concentrate on the garden. You can leave the car where it is."

"Miss Kenyon will expect me for lunch," Blair said regretfully.

"Call her up."

"There's no phone."

"Then drive out to tell her yourself. You can be back in twenty minutes. Oh, and Jerome's had a call from that tiresome sister of his so he won't be back tonight. Plan to have dinner with me. We'll make a day of it. Do you eat omelettes?"

"Love them." Blair drove back, smiling. Something about Emily Cook had dissipated like a breath of fresh air all the tensions of the morning.

She opened the door of the cottage. Nothing had been straightened. Her slippers were still on the floor in front of the fireplace. She picked them up and carried them into her own room. Through the open bathroom door she saw Ann Kenyon, again in worn jersey and slacks, busy at a typewriter in the room beyond.

"I'm lunching with Mrs. Cook," she called out, "and I won't be back to dinner."

The clatter of the typewriter stopped. "Oh? That's fine." Miss Kenyon began to type again as though she had already dismissed her boarder from her mind. Blair found herself hoping that Emily Cook would renew her invitation. It would be pleasant to live in that absurd, rambling house.

Emily was at the side door to greet her as she returned. "Gladys is a good cook but she refuses—and quite rightly, I think—to be hurried. She is making popovers. It will give me a chance to show you the house." She laughed. "And you mustn't think you have to be polite about it. I love it because Jerome wanted it this way but I'm perfectly aware that architecturally it is a horror."

It was a big house, to which wings had been added haphazardly and then left unfinished. Only half a dozen rooms were open for use, the furnishing lovely but worn and shabby. Emily could make an empty room feel as though a fire had been lighted on the hearth.

While they went from room to room, from wing to wing, Blair explained the purpose of her visit.

"Of course," Emily agreed readily, "I can give you a list of people who have good pieces for sale. In fact, I'll go with you this afternoon just to introduce you and start you off right. It will be great fun. Anyhow, there's," she looked uneasily at Blair, "a little antagonism."

"I know about it," Blair told her quietly, "and I think it is quite fantastic. Actually," it did not occur to

her that she was being indiscreet, "that's why Mr. Potter came. To find out who is starting those rumors and
put an end to them."

"It is that unspeakable Paul Brooks," Emily said indignantly, "but there's no mystery about why he is
doing it. He wants the people in town to oppose the
Center so he can build his housing development. But
among us we'll settle his hash."

She sounded so fierce that Blair laughed at her and
Emily laughed back. "Anyhow," she said cheerfully,
"I'm delighted about one thing, that Glen got that station wagon. He has a phobia about driving and he refused to own a car. Now with all this scandal he is beginning to fight it by openly having a car. You are
going to be good for him, my dear."

When lunch was over Emily climbed into the station
wagon beside Blair. "Where would you like to go
first?"

"Who has the best stuff?"

"The Randalls," Emily said promptly. "Simply fabulous. But they are hopeless."

"Why are they?"

"Eccentrics. A brother and sister, nearly eighty.
They have furniture that goes back generations and
generations. In a way, they are slaves to it. They have
arthritis and ought to go to a warm sunny climate but
they won't leave their house and belongings."

"Tell me more about them," Blair said, her eyes
dancing with excitement.

"They were friends of my parents, strong on tradi-
tion, loyal, stiff-necked, admirable and exasperating."

"Let's try them."

"All right," Emily conceded, "but don't expect too
much. They have been refusing to let dealers in the
house for years, though their things are famous."

The Randalls had an old colonial house a mile or
two out of town. Miss Randall herself admitted them,
erect, stately, thin as a rail, with fingers swollen and
twisted by arthritis. Her face lighted as she saw Emily
and she ushered them through a hallway where Blair,

wide eyed, saw an early 1700 Hadley chest, into a room that made her gasp. Outside of the American Wing at the Metropolitan Museum she had never seen such pieces.

Emily chatted about the unpredictable weather, the deplorable neglect of the roads and the general decline of the caliber of politicians. It was Miss Randall who turned to Blair.

"So you are the young woman who has come to work for Glen. I've been hearing about you. What do you think about his project and what's your part in it?"

"I'm to run the antique shop and I think the whole idea is splendid. It's going to be the saving of this town."

"It's going to take a lot of money to persuade people to part with family treasures for that shop of his. And as he doesn't intend to profit himself, he's going to be pouring out money for sentimental reasons. And the whole idea is preposterous. It's one thing to keep your own family treasures, but for fools to buy other people's heirlooms is simply catering to their vulgarity."

Blair ignored Miss Randall's tart tone. "I think," she said quietly, "that you've missed the whole point of what Mr. Forbes is trying to do. It's something a lot more important than collecting heirlooms. He's trying to save the heritage of these people, create a kind of clearing house, help them to rediscover their old Yankee ingenuity which has begun to rust from lack of use."

"Glen has made an enthusiastic convert," the old woman said with a shrewd look at Blair. "Of course, the man has irresistible charm. If I were forty years younger—"

Blair ignored the personal comment. "It's more than that. It's not just a project he is fighting for, it's a way of life."

There was a glint of humor in the faded eyes. "Of course, you've come here to try to talk me out of my antiques."

Blair smiled. "Honestly, Miss Randall, can you think

of any better fate for them? Sold to people who will
value and cherish them, and at the same time help to
preserve the values for which they stand?"

"You are quite an advocate."

"Well," Blair pointed out, "either there will be the
Center, built on faith in these people, or there will be
Mr. Brooks' housing development built on a contempt
for people. That's the choice."

Miss Randall studied her for a moment and turned
to Emily Cook. "You know, Emily," she said candidly,
"they say the third time is lucky. This girl of Glen's—"

Blair's face burned. "But I'm not—"

"Nonsense, my dear, you are head over heels in love
with the man. If you don't know it, it's high time you
found it out. In any case, you're a fighter, and I like
that. Dan and I have been wanting to go to Arizona for
years. If we go we aren't likely to come back. I'd intended to present our furniture to a museum but I'm
wondering whether it wouldn't serve a better purpose
if Glen had it. Instead of a memorial to the past, it will,
perhaps, help to build the future. Now shall we look
around and see what you'd like to have for the shop?"

Three hours later, Blair put down her pen and flexed
her fingers. "That's the lot," she said. "When may I
send for the furniture?"

"In two weeks," Miss Randall said. "It took me
thirty years to make up my mind but now I can't wait
to go."

"I'll come with the men who pack it," Blair promised, "and supervise it myself."

When she and Emily were back at the Cooks' house,
she said, "I don't believe it. Do you realize that the
shop will be made? Off Madison Avenue there isn't—"

Emily squeezed her arm. "I knew you could handle
her if anyone could. Glen will be delighted. We'll have
to drink to this."

She mixed a pitcher of martinis and brought them
into the living room where Blair was poring over her
list. The girl reached blindly for her glass. "Do you realize," she said, her voice dazed, "that just what Miss

Randall called the junk in that big shed is terribly in
demand? Lazy Susans, pie safes, dry sinks—people
love them! And as for—"

Emily laughed. "Put down that list and drink your
martini. I'm cook at night. You rest while I get
dinner."

"Let's have our drinks in the kitchen and I'll help,"
Blair volunteered. "I'm too excited to rest."

Emily lifted her glass. "Here's to you and your fabulous *coup*. I'm terribly glad you've come and I hope
you'll stay. Glen has put so much of himself into the
Center and he's been so—alone. He needs someone to
share his enthusiasm. No one has ever really done that.
Oh, both Connie and Evelyn tried but, for some reason
that escapes me, Glen, who is really a sensible man,
married two silly women. He married Connie because
everyone expected him to and Evelyn—well, in my
opinion, he married her for the worst reason in the
world—pity. The worst possible foundation for marriage," she went on emphatically. "After all, what happens to pity for other people after self-pity crops up?
Well, it's one thing no one takes advice on. I didn't
myself when I married Jerome. But when you're infatuated you don't listen and I'm so glad I didn't. Do have
another drink. They aren't strong."

Dinner passed in a spate of talk that flowed easily
between the two women who liked each other. Afterwards, Emily stacked the dishes and left them for
Gladys and showed Blair an old album that contained
pictures of some antiques that might, with a little diplo-
macy, be acquired.

Blair turned the pages idly. There was a wedding
picture of Glen Forbes some years younger and a tall
arrogant dark girl with a sensual mouth.

"Connie Brooks," Emily said. "Glen's first wife."
Her tone, for Emily, was carefully noncommittal.
Much farther on there was a snapshot of a small thin
girl with pale hair, wistful eyes and drooping mouth.
"Evelyn Harrison," Emily said. "Poor thing."

Among the snapshots was one of a man laughing,

his head flung back. So that was what Glen Forbes was like when he was happy.

"Charlie, of course," Emily said.

"I thought it was his cousin."

"They're so alike and so different. Charlie is a lovable creature, irresponsible but lovable. And utterly devoted to Glen. He drinks too much and it's not good for him. He ought to marry and settle down. He's—accident prone. That—the way he nearly ran you down—he must feel awful about it."

"He does," Blair said. "But it could have happened to anyone."

"That's what I say," Emily answered quickly. "It could have happened to anyone."

It was nearly eleven when Blair left Emily Cook and drove back to Miss Kenyon's cottage. She dreaded the forthcoming interview and her landlady's embarrassment. To her relief the house was dark. Miss Kenyon had gone to bed, as reluctant as herself for a meeting. She unlocked the door and fumbled for the switch.

Light burned in Miss Kenyon's room. Blair listened but there was no sound. Walking on tiptoe she went into the room. Miss Kenyon lay in bed, asleep and drunk. On the bedside table there was an empty glass and a bottle of whisky.

Blair was thoughtful as she went to bed. If Emily Cook did not repeat her invitation, she would have to tell her that Miss Kenyon's drinking was chronic.

That night she slept heavily. Once she stirred as a truck rattled by. But there were no trucks on this road, she remembered. No one lived there but Miss Kenyon. Once she awakened, thinking a light had shone on her face, but the room was dark. She lay rigid, listening, but the sound of her own pounding heart covered any other sound, if there were any other sound.

After a while a floor board creaked. Perhaps Miss Kenyon was sick again. Miss Kenyon muttered something and set the glass down hard on the table. More whisky. Blair slid down in bed and this time she slept without disturbance.

12

The alarm jolted Blair awake. Again she had to prepare her own breakfast. Before leaving the house she paused at Miss Kenyon's door. The light still burned. Miss Kenyon lay still. Something about her posture disturbed the girl and she moved forward, closer to the bed. There was no rise and fall of the chest in breathing. Miss Kenyon was really horribly quiet.

Blair bent over the bed. Miss Kenyon's jaw had dropped. Through half-open lids her eyes looked up sightlessly. Miss Kenyon was dead.

For a long horrified moment Blair stared down at the woman on the bed. Then, reluctantly, she touched the white cheek with her fingertips. It was cold. She must have been dead a long time.

What had happened? Had her landlady had a heart attack? Or did people die of alcoholism? But she had not been that drunk. Or did that matter? Blair felt a stab of pity. To die like that, alone, sordidly in the dark. No, she remembered, at least she had had the light, but it would be of no comfort in the darkness into which she had gone.

I've got to get help, the girl thought. If only there were a telephone! She caught up her coat, locked the door behind her and climbed into the station wagon. She had difficulty with the key and realized that she was shaking.

She started the motor and turned carefully in the muddy lane. Back through the bridge again. The clattering of the car over loose floorboards reminded her of the sound she had taken for a truck passing the cottage in the night. Of course, it had been a car going through the bridge.

Her heart sank when she saw there was no smoke curling from the chimney at the Center. She had counted on Forbes being awake, taking charge. She sounded the horn and then got out to hammer on the door of the salt box. There was no answer.

At length, she climbed back into the car, close to panic. What on earth was she to do? She could hardly go to Emily Cook with her problem, involve a stranger, a woman whom she had met only two days before, in Miss Kenyon's sordid death. If Mr. Potter had been on hand—but he had gone to New York. No help there.

Thinking of the silent body stiffening on the bed she roused herself. She had to do something, get help somewhere. She drove into town and drew up at the curb beside the drugstore where a man was unlocking the door.

He turned in surprise, a middle-aged man with a placid face. "You're bright and early. No coffee for ten minutes."

"It's an emergency," Blair told him. "My landlady is dead and I've got to notify someone."

He gave a quick look at her face and then held open the door for her. When he had switched on the lights he indicated the telephone booth in the rear. She started toward it, paused uncertainly.

"I don't know whom to call."

"Stranger, here?"

"Yes, I just came day before yesterday."

"Had she any family?"

"I don't know, but I'm pretty sure there's no one in Bridgetown."

"Who is her physician?"

"I don't know. She may not have had anyone. She had been here only a few months herself."

"Dr. Huger is the best man but he's at the hospital doing an emergency operation. Call Dr. Crothers, 3-124."

Blair fumbled with the dial while the druggist watched her.

"Here," he offered, "I'll do that." He pointed to a stool at the soda fountain. "Sit there. I'll mix some ammonia in a moment. If you feel faint, put your head down."

Blair climbed onto the stool while the druggist dialed the number and spoke briefly. He turned around. "What's the name and where does she live?"

"Miss Ann Kenyon. She has the brown cottage across the covered bridge and down the dirt road to the right. But I'll lead the way. I have to go back anyhow, because I locked the door and all my clothes are there."

The druggist came back to mix and push toward her a small glass containing a milky liquid. "Drink that. Dr. Crothers will pick you up here in ten minutes."

Blair drank the ammonia, slid off the stool and steadied herself for a moment against the counter. "I have to make a New York call," she said, and the obliging druggist gave her a handful of coins in exchange for a bill.

She sat in the booth waiting. At length she heard Mr. Potter's quiet and comforting voice.

"This is Blair Masters. I'm terribly sorry to bother you so early but something rather upsetting has happened and I don't quite know what to do."

Mr. Potter's voice indicated that a lady in distress was a perfectly normal situation.

"It's Miss Kenyon," she explained. "When I got up this morning she was still in bed. Before leaving the house I looked in her room. She's dead, Mr. Potter. She must have died in her sleep. I came back to town and I'm calling from a drugstore. I'm waiting for a doctor now."

Mr. Potter was silent for so long that she thought the connection had been broken. Then he said, "Don't try to stay there, Miss Masters. I'll call Mrs. Brenning and arrange for you to go to her house until I get back later this morning. Then we'll make better arrangements."

Dr. Crothers was a big man, tall and wide, with gray hair, unpressed clothes and a defeated manner.

"You the young lady? We'd better get going. She may still be alive."

Blair shook her head. "She's dead."

"Have you had much experience with death?"

"No, but—"

"Then you can't be sure."

Blair led the way in the station wagon while the doctor trailed her in a shabby sedan. When they reached the cottage she unlocked the door and pointed out Miss Kenyon's room. Then she went into her own room and began to pack her bags.

A quarter of an hour passed before Dr. Crothers came into her room. He gave Blair a sharp look. "I can't sign a certificate."

Blair was as startled by his manner as by his words. "What's wrong?"

He answered her question with another, "Why did you wait so long to report the death?"

"But I didn't," she explained. "I didn't know until I looked in this morning. As soon as I found her I drove right into town to report it and get help."

"You had to turn on the light to see her?" he asked, his eyes straying toward the daylight that brightened the room.

"She left the light. She's afraid to go to sleep in the dark."

Weary, skeptical eyes summed her up, diagnosing her case, Blair thought wildly.

"Is she the Miss Kenyon who's a writer?"

Blair nodded.

"Are you the young lady who came here to work for Glen Forbes?"

She nodded again.

Dr. Crothers pulled at his lower lip. "Are you trying to make me believe," he said nastily, "that you live here and yet you didn't see this woman until a few minutes ago? That you didn't so much as look in there?"

The open hostility in his voice angered Blair. "Of course I looked in. Last night when I came home. She was asleep and there was a bottle of whisky beside her bed."

There was frank incredulity in his expression. "Oh, come now! You didn't know that she was dead?" His short laugh held so much suspicion that she was staggered.

"Dead! But she couldn't have been. She—" Blair broke off. "She couldn't—" She sank down on the side of her bed, staring at him, trying to remember. "She was breathing last night," she exclaimed. "I remember distinctly. "And she was alive much later—maybe two o'clock—because I heard her mutter and she took a drink."

His eyes never left her face. "And it didn't even enter your head to call a doctor then?"

"But she was just drunk. I thought she'd sleep it off. She had been very drunk the night before, passed out at a dinner party, and she was sick in the night. But she was all right next morning."

"Sick in the night," he repeated alertly. "How sick?"

Blair told him.

"What did you give her?"

"A glass of water."

"Just water," he said queerly. "Well, you looked in at her last night and she was asleep."

"Yes."

It was obvious that he did not believe her. Blair supposed, confusedly, that he thought she had been afraid of death, that she had run away from it.

Someone came up on the porch. Blair opened the door to find Stanley Brenning frowning at her.

"What's all this, Miss Masters?" he demanded abruptly. "Hiram Potter telephoned from New York—oh, good morning, doctor. Is Miss Kenyon really—?"

Dr. Crothers's inexplicable hostility faded at the sight of Brenning. His manner became almost ingratiating. "I was explaining to the young lady that I can't give a certificate."

Brenning stood motionless. Then he turned to Blair. "You are to come home with me, Miss Masters. My wife is expecting you. Suppose we let you go on with your packing."

He took the doctor's arm and led him out of the room, closing the door behind him.

Blair packed quickly, aware of the woman who lay so still in the next room, of the murmur of voices from the living room. Once, when she went into the bathroom for her toothbrush, she thought she heard the two men in the room next door.

When she had finished packing she carried her bags out to the living room. The men broke off a low-toned conversation. Brenning helped her put her luggage in the station wagon, locked the door of the house, and led the little procession of three cars as they drove slowly away.

When they reached the big house on the hill, Blair was so dazed by shock that she was only vaguely aware of Mrs. Brenning, in a heavy quilted robe that made her look almost square, bombarding her with eager questions. She had begun to shake again.

"No questions now, Beulah," her husband said sharply. "Miss Masters has had a shock. Doctor, perhaps you can give her something to quiet her."

After a startled look at her husband, Mrs. Brenning took Blair up to a guest room where she dropped down on the bed. In a few moments the doctor came in with a white tablet and a glass of water. When he had gone, she lay quiet, staring at the ceiling. Her fingers touched the cool surface of the pillow case and she jerked them away, remembering the chilly cheek of Miss Kenyon.

Cold air from the open window made her eyes sting and she closed them, half awake, half asleep. Once more she was beating at the door of Forbes' house. But the house had changed. It was Bluebeard's secret chamber she was trying to open. Then she was jerked to one side as a car's brakes screamed and Charlie told her, "I don't remember, but Glen says I did it." The voice went on and on, as relentlessly as rain, "Glen says I did it. Glen says I did it." And then someone laughed jeeringly, "Head over heels in love with the man." Her lips parted to protest, "But it isn't—" and no words would come out.

When she awakened, the room was dusky with rain falling in gusts from a gray sky. She answered a soft tap at the door and a maid came in with a tray which she set on a table. She gave Blair a look of avid curiosity and the girl stumbled to her feet, groggy, aware of mussed clothes, of tousled hair.

"Mrs. Brenning is sorry to disturb you but Mr. Potter would like to see you as soon as possible."

"Mr. Potter!" Blair exclaimed. "What time is it?"

"Eleven-thirty, miss."

"Good heavens!" Blair poured coffee while she tried to rouse herself to the realities of the day. "Will you telephone to Mr. Glen Forbes at the Center and say that I'll be very late. I'll explain when I see him."

"I guess he already knows," the maid blurted out. "Or else he's the only one in town who doesn't." She lingered for a moment. "You're the one who found her, aren't you, miss?"

"Yes," Blair said briefly.

After another curious glance, the maid went out reluctantly, and closed the door behind her.

II

Mr. Potter had spent an idle afternoon. At this point there was nothing he could do but await reports from Sam Trumble and Opal Reed, the one on Joan Brenning's present activities, the other on Ann Kenyon's past activities. Hounded by a feeling of anxiety, he was in no mood for idleness. He indulged in a recital at Town Hall, which proved to be an error in judgment, for the novice soprano had learned to run before she had learned to walk. There were moments when one caught a glimpse of the voice she had had before singing teachers got hold of it, but the rest was sheer discomfort.

To compensate himself, he drifted into his favorite record dealer's where he carried on an amiable warfare, as the dealer had never heard the phrase about the customer always being right. Any such illusions he dealt with firmly. But as he had a disconcerting habit of being right Mr. Potter submitted cheerfully to being bullied and browbeaten into buying records which he inevitably enjoyed. This time he bore off triumphantly some recordings of Badora-Skoda playing Mozart, whose cool limpid loveliness would banish the memory of the inept singer.

Then, lest he become too self-indulgent, for he had been brought up by a mother who had taught him that every pleasure must be paid for, he strolled down Irving Place to the Sleepy Hollow Bookshop where he picked up the latest Kenyon book, considerably to the surprise of the proprietor. Fortified by a couple of martinis and one of Antonia's excellent dinners, he sat down to read.

The writing was better than he had expected. The pace was good. The sense of reality was always present. But the atmosphere was murky, with a brooding fascination in the sheer fact of violence, a kind of gloating over detailed descriptions of physical pain. And always, like an undercurrent, ran terror; accounted for by the report Opal Reed had given him over the telephone from Elmwood.

When he had finished the book, Mr. Potter closed it and sat tapping the cover thoughtfully, thinking of an impressionable young girl watching in paralyzed horror while her father strangled her mother. No wonder she had become distorted; no wonder she had turned to alcohol to blot out unendurable memories. Obviously she was driven by a need for revenge, in writing her books. But the point remained: who had put her on the track of the Bridgetown murders? From what Blair had reported of her conversation with the drunken woman, it seemed possible that she herself had not known for sure the identity of the person who had brought her to Bridgetown until the fatal dinner party. What was it she had said? Mr. Potter tried to remember the words but they eluded him.

The more he thought of the dinner the more it bothered him. Miss Kenyon had been asking for trouble. He struggled into his topcoat, took the key and let himself into Gramercy Park where he paced up and down the gravel paths, hands in his pockets.

He watched the lights in the high buildings around the park blink out one by one, watched the diminishing flow of traffic until only a trickle of taxis moved with the changing green and red lights, and an occasional fire engine with the wailing siren that, like Emily Dickinson's snake, left zero at the bone. He turned to the west and saw, looming high above his own house, the office building from which, a year before, a girl had plunged to her death in his own garden. He shivered. Sick at heart he let himself out of the park, heard the iron gate clang behind him, and went home to bed.

He slept badly and when Tito knocked at his door in the morning he had already showered and shaved and was putting on his shoes.

"Miss Masters is on the telephone."

He heard Blair Masters' voice. Too high. Too tense. Ann Kenyon was dead; she had died in her sleep.

When he had set down the telephone Mr. Potter looked blankly at the wall. I did that, he thought. Always the catalytic agent. If I hadn't got Blair the job with Forbes and asked Mrs. Brenning to invite the Kenyon woman to dinner, she would be alive now.

Not for a moment did he allow himself to hope that it had been a natural death. She had revealed herself at the dinner party as a source of danger and she had had to be silenced before she said anything more. But whether the danger was to Forbes or someone who was framing Forbes, he did not know.

Grimly he called Brenning in Bridgetown, explained

the situation and asked him to take charge of Blair. Brenning, incredulous, sputtering, alarmed, agreed to do so at once. When he had broken the connection, Mr. Potter telephoned Forbes at the Center. The phone rang again and again before the operator said, "They do not answer."

Then, through information, he got Paul Brooks' house. Again there was no reply. At length he called Jerome Cook and got a startled Emily.

"This is Hiram Potter and terribly sorry to disturb you."

"Potter? Oh, yes, of course. Glen's good friend."

Mr. Potter's eyebrows arched. Who had been talking? "I'm trying to reach your cousin, Charlie Forbes. Can you give me his number?"

"Charlie?" He could hear the alarm in her voice. "There's nothing wrong, is there? Nothing's happened?" She gave him the number.

"Sorry I had to wake you so early."

"Oh, I wasn't asleep," Emily assured him. "When Jerome isn't here I always get up at dawn. There never seems to be time enough for a garden in the spring. Jerome's tiresome sister is ill again and the poor lamb had to go to Stamford to see her."

When he had thanked Emily, leaving her questions unanswered, Mr. Potter called Charlie's number. Again no answer. He sat staring at the telephone. Four of a kind, he thought glumly. Not one of the men is available.

One thing, only one thing, emerged clearly from the whole situation. Untenable as Glen Forbes' position had been before, it would be impossible now. Miss Kenyon's dinner conversation would become public property. What Forbes needed at this point was not a friend; not even a detective. It was a lawyer—and a miracle.

As soon as Sam's report came in, he would pick up Joan and get back to Bridgetown. He would find out where all four men had been when Miss Kenyon died. For the first time he found himself hoping that Forbes was the man with Joan. At least, whatever his emotional involvement, he would be cleared of a graver charge. In any case, Mr. Potter would advise Forbes to get a lawyer, a more adequate and less timid man than Brenning. And he would send Blair Masters home.

I killed Miss Kenyon as surely as though I'd put a pistol to her head and pulled the trigger, he told himself. So help me God, I'll never interfere in anyone's troubles again.

The telephone rang sharply and he jumped. "Hello . . . Oh, yes, Sam."

"I muffed it," Sam said disconsolately. "They just left here but I couldn't see the guy's face. Gray felt hat and gray overcoat. Registered as Alvin Owen of Baltimore. Maryland license plates." He gave the number. "You can't call me anything I've overlooked."

"Spilt milk," Mr. Potter said philosophically. "At least, we've got the license number and it may help yet. Talk to the manager. Someone must have seen the fellow when he arrived."

"I've already talked to her. The girl was on the lookout and waved to him as he drove up. He never went near the office."

Mr. Potter looked up Kurt Tyson's number and dialed. "Thank God, you're on hand early."

"Not early," the detective grumbled, "late. Just finished a report on a big job." He yawned. "What's on your mind?" He listened while Mr. Potter explained what he wanted.

"I'll check on the license plates," Tyson said at last, "though I can't see what they've got to do with the Bridgetown murders, except that they might eliminate one suspect. What are you running into up there— mass murder?"

"I don't know," Mr. Potter admitted.

"You get yourself into the damnedest things," Tyson remarked dispassionately. "You seem to breed murder."

"That," Mr. Potter told him soberly, "is what I've been thinking."

13

When Mr. Potter entered the lobby of the Plaza Joan Brenning was waiting for him. There were shadows under her eyes from fatigue and the eyes themselves had a glazed, unfocused look. The excitement had burned out, but her lips, which had always been so thin, seemed fuller, warmer. He wondered in some consternation whether she had any suspicion of how much her telltale face would reveal to her watchful and alarmed mother, but he realized that Joan had gone a long way in the past twenty-four hours. She was too happy to care.

They were both silent as the car rolled north on the parkways, Mr. Potter busy with his thoughts, Joan half asleep. Now and then he shot her a sidewise glance. At length he said, "You know, Joan, if you want to avoid some awkward questions when you get home, you had better stop looking like the cat that swallowed the canary. Wipe those feathers off your lips."

She gave him a startled look and then, to his surprise, she blushed deeply.

"There's always a chance," he went on, "on one of these little escapades of yours, that your parents might telephone the Plaza. You might at least register there."

"You nasty little spy!" she said furiously.

Mr. Potter made no comment but he had an impression that behind her fury there was fear.

When she spoke her voice was sullen, "How did you find out?"

"A mutual friend happened to be staying at the same

motel last night. Who is Mr. Owen of Baltimore?"

As soon as he had spoken, he knew that he had blundered. The alarm died out of her face. She smiled maliciously.

"Don't you wish you knew?"

"I wish to God you'd watch your step."

"I know what I'm doing. I can take care of myself."

"No woman," he pointed out, "can rely very far or very long on the man who takes her to a motel under an assumed name. Don't be more of a fool than you can help. And, by the way, if that is what you had in mind when you suggested that I play along, you miscalculated. I'm not going to take any responsibility for this. So far as I am concerned the age of chivalry is dead and knighthood is no longer in flower. No shotgun marriages for Potter."

"I wouldn't have you as a gift," she said coldly. "You needn't worry."

"Good!" His approval was wholehearted. "That's mutual."

"Do you intend to do a sneak and tell my parents?" His silence shamed her. "Sorry, I shouldn't have said that but it makes me do a slow burn to have people checking up on me."

"You might as well get used to it," Mr. Potter said. "I have an impression that there is going to be a lot of checking up from now on in Bridgetown. Things have been happening there while we were gone and I suspect that a number of people will want an accounting for our time."

"What do you mean?"

"Ann Kenyon is dead."

"Kenyon!" Joan turned to him blankly. "The writing woman? The way you say it—you mean someone murdered her?"

"I'm afraid so."

"But why would anyone do that? Oh—I suppose you mean Glen. Or Charlie trying to protect Glen. But I can't see Charlie killing someone for Glen's sake, can you? He thinks Glen is perfect but he'd hardly do his killing for him. And Glen, the cold fish, wouldn't bother."

"You jump at conclusions, don't you?" Mr. Potter remarked mildly. "You can get into trouble doing that."

"Whatever I do you think I'm headed for trouble," Joan scoffed.

"I know you are." His very lack of emphasis silenced her for some time.

"Well," she said at last, "whatever happens, just let me handle my own problems by myself. That's all I ask." Her good humor had returned. She slipped her hand confidingly under his arm. "You'd be rather a darling if you weren't such an old maid."

"Save it," he told her.

When he drove up to the Brenning house Mrs. Brenning herself flung open the door. "Thank heavens, you are back!"

"Miss Masters?" Mr. Potter asked quickly.

"Stanley brought her here this morning and the doctor gave her a sedative. She is still resting. She was so dazed we thought she had better sleep as long as possible. And Stanley wants you to go to his office at once. Before you see or talk to anyone. He said to be sure and impress that on you. Before you see or talk to anyone."

She met a penetrating blue gaze and turned to Joan. "I'm so glad my little girl was away when all this unpleasantness happened. Did you have a nice time?"

Joan's lips twitched. "Very nice."

Mrs. Brenning scanned her daughter's face and her eyes widened, her color drained away. Before she could speak Joan ran lightly up the stairs to her own room. Her mother turned to Mr. Potter, an anguished question trembling on her lips.

He forestalled her. "I'll go down to see Mr. Brenning now. When Miss Masters wakes up please ask her to stay here until I return. I want to talk to her. I hope all this is not inconveniencing you too terribly. I'll make some other arrangements for her today."

"I hope," Mrs. Brenning said tartly, "that she appreciates all you are doing for her. These ambitious young career women are apt to be out for all they can get."

Mr. Potter grinned. "I'll be off, as Mr. Brenning seems to be in a great hurry."

Something in his tone made her say defensively, "Stanley is Glen Forbes' lawyer, you know. Naturally, he's almost frantic."

"You must not be in too much of a hurry to condemn Forbes. After all, he may—just possibly—not have killed the woman."

When he reached Brenning's office the lawyer bounced up from his big chair with a sigh of relief. "Come in, Potter. I see Beulah gave you my message. I take it you haven't talked to anyone."

"I came here at once," Mr. Potter assured him, settled himself comfortably and waited with the composure of a man who has limitless time at his disposal.

"That's good. Did Joan come back with you?"

Mr. Potter's brows arched in mild surprise. "Of course."

"Now, Hiram," Brenning said, studying the palm of his left hand as though he expected to read his fortune on it, "it's always easiest to stop trouble right at the source. This morning, when you telephoned, you said, in the heat of excitement, that Miss Kenyon had been killed. That's dangerous talk. The kind of thing that quite easily can lead to trouble. Actually, the poor woman had a heart attack. Dr. Crothers is making out the death certificate."

"Dr. Crothers," Mr. Potter commented, "seems to be a friend of yours."

Brenning controlled his temper with a visible effort. "Because of your unfortunate personal experience, your views are naturally highly colored, a bit melodramatic, but there is no evidence that Miss Kenyon's death was not due to natural causes."

Mr. Potter leaned forward. "Mr. Brenning, night before last at your own dining table that woman simply asked to be murdered. And now I'm expected to believe that, at the most convenient moment, she has obligingly died a natural death. Well, I don't believe it. You can't protect a murderer."

"There is no evidence that there was a murder." Mr. Brenning appeared to take great satisfaction in this phrase.

"And if there had been any evidence, you are making sure that it won't come to light."

"For God's sake, man," Brenning exploded, "whose side are you on? Glen told me in confidence he had asked you to come up here and help him straighten out this mess. Do you want to send him to the electric chair?"

Mr. Potter studied him thoughtfully. "So you think Glen killed her."

"I didn't say that," Brenning protested. "I don't even allow myself to think it. But there's no escaping the fact that no one else has any motive. If a rumor gets out, suggesting that there's any mystery about Kenyon's death, Glen will be finished. The town is already against him and in an ugly temper, the kind of mood that might even lead to mob violence. The woman is dead. Let the thing rest there."

"It can't rest there," Mr. Potter pointed out patiently. "Three women have died by violence. Unless we act fast, there's no guarantee that there won't be a fourth or a fifth." His eyes held the older man's. "You can't get away with this."

"What do you want to do?" Brenning's sullen tone reminded Mr. Potter of Joan.

"Find out the truth," he answered promptly. "Find out who killed those three women. Stop the murderer before he can kill again."

"So you think Glen's wives were murdered."

"So do you," Mr. Potter told him.

"And I thought—Glen thought—that you were his friend."

"So much his friend," Mr. Potter retorted, "that I

am ready to give him a hearing before I condemn him."

"No one else will," Brenning said heavily. "I can tell you that. No one else will. One word about this and Glen might as well shoot himself. And not only that." Brenning studied the other palm. "Dr. Crothers can't figure why Miss Masters waited until morning to report that something was wrong with Miss Kenyon. He simply doesn't believe her story."

"What did kill the woman?" Mr. Potter asked.

Brenning capitulated with a helpless gesture. "Sleeping pills." He added almost pleadingly, "She'd had too much to drink. It could have been an accident. Even suicide."

"What about the evidence?"

"There was a drinking glass beside her bed with sediment in it. Some barbiturate."

"Where is it now?"

"Dr. Crothers took it with him."

Mr. Potter's brows arched. "What have you got on your tame doctor?"

"A mortgage on his house. He's had a bad time of it, a sick wife for years who was nothing but a drain; a son who died leaving a lot of debts. He's an easy-going man who fell behind the procession. He doesn't have much of a practice any more, just about enough to pay expenses, and he's tired, he doesn't want any trouble."

"He's taking a damned poor way of keeping out of trouble," Mr. Potter retorted. "And you are taking a short-sighted way of protecting Forbes' interests. Assuming his innocence—if that isn't too big a strain—he has everything to gain by clearing up Miss Kenyon's death instead of hushing it up."

"It's too big a chance," Brenning said. "I'm afraid to take it."

Mr. Potter stared out of the window at the rain. At length he said, "Did you look through Miss Kenyon's things?"

"Certainly not," the lawyer said virtuously.

Mr. Potter's imp danced in his eyes. "It's unfortunate that your respect for the law assails you at the wrong time. Who has the key to her house?"

After considerable vacillation Brenning drew out the doorkey and flung it across the desk. "I hope to God you know what you are doing."

Mr. Potter ignored the lawyer's groan of protest. "There's one thing more. Call Dr. Crothers and tell him I'm on my way. You might prepare the ground for me."

II

Dr. Crothers' office was in his house with a separate entrance around at the side. The house needed repainting and the porch steps needed mending. There were only two patients, both elderly women, in the shabby waiting room. Dust lay on the unswept carpet, on the arms of the chairs.

After a few moments Dr. Crothers opened an inner door, escorting a patient, and beckoned to the next. His eyelids flickered as he caught sight of Mr. Potter though he pretended, unsuccessfully, to ignore him.

Three quarters of an hour later, when the patients had gone, the doctor admitted Mr. Potter to his office, took off a grimy white coat and filled his pipe.

"Well?" he said, a challenge in his voice.

Mr. Potter smiled faintly. "It's hardly well, is it? Believe me, doctor, you will find in the long run that I am doing you a service. Sooner or later, the death of Miss Kenyon is bound to be investigated. When that time comes, you'd be in a damnably awkward position if you had issued the death certificate. The least it could do would be to affect your professional standing."

Dr. Crothers took a long breath. "I signed the certificate this morning," he said in the tone of a man who has burned his boats.

"So that's that. That means no autopsy. No official investigation." At length Mr. Potter broke the silence. "Well, you don't deserve to be protected, you know.

And there's a limit to what Brenning can do for you. How many sleeping pills did she get?"

As the doctor made no reply he went on, "I realize, of course, we can't get anything but approximations without an autopsy. But you must have a fair idea."

"It was a lethal dose."

"How long had she been dead when you saw her?"

"A couple of hours, more or less. I must point out, of course, that the window was wide open and it was a chilly night."

"Look here, doctor, accustomed as you must be to death, doesn't it bother you at all to know a woman has been put out of the way quite ruthlessly? To know that her murderer is free to strike again?"

Dr. Crothers smiled sarcastically. "I understand from Mr. Brenning that you are trying to help Glen Forbes clear up the rumors about his wives' deaths, that you produced this girl Friday of his. I can tell you this for your own satisfaction. The person who had the best chance to administer those sleeping pills was the girl. And she was damned careful to wait until it was too late to save the woman before she sounded the alarm. If any questions come up, I'd have to testify to that."

"It's an interesting theory," Mr. Potter agreed politely. "The only trouble with it is that it's not true. The girl never met Forbes until she came here two days ago. She's not so insane that she would commit a murder for him. It occurs to me, doctor, that before making any more threats you would be well advised to help us solve the death according to the evidence rather than according to your prejudices. And now about that drinking glass. Did you handle it?"

The doctor opened a white porcelain case and showed him a glass with a white sediment in the bottom. A thermometer was standing in it. "I picked it up with this," he explained. "Never touched the glass."

"We'll start by having this stuff analyzed and check the glass for fingerprints. We've got to know, not guess."

Mr. Potter wrapped the glass in cardboard, careful not to handle it or blur any marks that might be on it, and took it away with him. He took, too, a look of startled speculation in the doctor's eyes.

When Mr. Potter got back to the Brenning house he caught sight of his hostess strategically seated in the immense drawing room where she had a view of the main hall. She did not intend to let him pass without an accounting for the time he and Joan had spent in New York. To his relief, Blair Masters came down the stairs before she could hail him.

"Get a raincoat, will you, Miss Masters, and come for a ride? I hope you don't mind a little weather. I'll tell Mrs. Brenning you are lunching with me."

Blair hesitated. "I really ought to explain to Mr. Forbes."

"We'll stop at the Center together." While she went back to her room he told Mrs. Brenning that Blair would be lunching with him.

"You won't stir up any trouble, will you, Hiram?" she asked anxiously.

"Don't you think," he said gently, "that someone else has done that?"

The older woman's face hardened. "Let's understand each other, Hiram. Stanley telephoned me after you left him. You intend to make trouble, but do you understand clearly the kind of trouble you'll be making? There was no one with Miss Kenyon last night but the Masters girl. You work out the answer."

He nodded his fair head, gave her a bland and unrevealing look and turned to smile at Blair as she came down the stairs wearing a red raincoat with a hood pulled down over her dark hair.

He drove slowly away from the house, turned onto a deserted dirt lane and stopped the car. For a moment they sat in silence, listening to the rain drumming on the top, watching it stream down the windshield.

"Now then," he said, "tell me all about it. Take your time and don't leave out anything."

"Where do I start?"

"When I left you at Miss Kenyon's cottage night before last."

"But I told you about that at the Center yesterday morning."

"Tell me again. Everything."

Obediently Blair described being awakened by Miss Kenyon's nausea, how she had put her to bed, exactly what had been said.

"You brought her a glass of water. What happened then?"

"She drank a little and I put it down on the table beside her bed."

"You didn't see any sleeping pills in the medicine closet, did you?"

Blair's eyes widened. "Is that what—?"

Mr. Potter nodded.

"I didn't see them because they weren't there. She had nothing in the medicine chest but toothpaste and mouthwash and shampoo and bicarbonate of soda. Not even aspirin. She said she didn't believe in drugs. No, Mr. Potter, there must be some mistake. She couldn't have taken sleeping pills."

"Well, let it go for the moment. Tell me about yesterday."

Blair described the day from the interview with Brenning and renting the station wagon, to her trip with Emily Cook, the fabulous antiques she had acquired, the evening's celebration and her return home at night. Miss Kenyon had already gone to bed and she was drunk again. There was a bottle of whisky and a glass beside her bed.

"Go on. Did anything happen in the night?"

"I heard her put down the glass." Blair described being aroused by what she had taken for a truck and later had realized was a car going through the covered bridge. After that she had thought a light flashed in her eyes, she heard a board creak, a mutter, the sound of the glass being set down.

"Go on."

"This morning I looked in her room. She was dead."

Blair was very white. "Mr. Potter, if I had tried to
rouse her last night, called the doctor then, would it
have saved her? I know he must think that. My only
excuse is that I don't know much about drunkenness. I
thought she'd sleep it off. It has been like a nightmare,
from the moment Dr. Crothers saw her. He simply
wouldn't believe I hadn't known something was wrong
last night. He was really hostile. He seemed to think
that I was afraid of death and had run off in a panic
and then lied about it. But then Mr. Brenning came
and everything was all right."

Mr. Potter turned in the seat to face her. "Brace
yourself, Blair," he said grimly. "Everything is about as
wrong as it could possibly be. Miss Kenyon was deliberately murdered with an overdose of sleeping pills dissolved in that glass of water. Dr. Crothers knows it and
so does Stanley Brenning, who silenced the doctor and
extorted that death certificate from him. The doctor
more than suspects you of having administered the fatal dose yourself."

Blair's lips opened, closed again. She looked at him
from dazed, incredulous eyes. "But why? I didn't even
know her."

"In your capacity as Forbes' employee, working for
his interests."

"But that—" she pushed back the hood of her raincoat and ran her fingers through her hair. "I can't take
it in. The whole thing is grotesque. It's monstrous.
Murder! Me!" The stunned look faded. Twin candles
flamed suddenly in her extraordinarily lovely eyes.
"This," she said through set teeth, "I'll fight if it's the
last thing I ever do."

"You understand," Mr. Potter said, "none of this
unsavory story is supposed to be made public. Dr.
Crothers has signed the certificate and committed himself. Brenning won't talk because it's his job to protect
Forbes."

"But he didn't—but I didn't—"

"I know you didn't."

"So what are you going to do?" she asked.

"What choice have I?" groaned Mr. Potter. "I am bitterly sorry—words aren't adequate to say how sorry I am to involve you any further in this ugly mess—but I've got to go ahead and find out the truth."

"Well, I should think so!"

He looked at her doubtfully. "Regardless?"

"Regardless," she declared. "We'll fight it out on this line if it takes all summer."

"We may not have that much time," he said. "I have a growing feeling that time is running out."

14

"Where do we begin?" Blair asked.

"We'll go to the Center," Mr. Potter decided, "and tell Forbes you won't be working today. I'd also like to know where he was yesterday and last night. I'd like that very much."

It did not seem that Blair could grow any paler. "I don't believe it," she choked. "He didn't kill her. He—Mr. Potter, that light that shone in my eyes, was that—whoever did it?"

"Well, someone got in that house last night."

"But how could he force her to take so many sleeping pills?"

"She was drunk," he reminded her. "They were probably dissolved in whisky. No trick to it."

Forbes was in his office when they drove up to the Center. He leaped to his feet as they appeared, his eyes moving from Mr. Potter to Blair.

"Emily called a few minutes ago," he told Blair. "She had heard a rumor that Miss Kenyon was dead. She has been trying to find you. She says you are to move over there at once. If you don't come she's going to fetch you."

"That's very kind of her," Blair said in relief, "and I accept with gratitude."

"It's true, then?"

Blair shivered. "Oh, yes, it's true. I found her."

"Suppose," Mr. Potter said, "I tell it."

When he had finished, Forbes ran his fingers through his hair. "There's no doubt in your mind that she was deliberately murdered?"

"No doubt at all. She didn't have any sleeping pills in the house. She didn't approve of drugs. Anyhow, she was at work on a book and planning to go ahead with it. There is no apparent motive for suicide. But there was a motive for murder."

"To prevent her from writing her book," Forbes agreed. "Obviously."

"Or to prevent her from revealing who brought her here in the first place," Mr. Potter said. "It seems evident that someone told her about the Bridgetown murders to get her here to help stress the fact that you are a murderer. But whoever it was may not have known until the dinner party that she's a chronic drunk and therefore dangerous. And there's no getting around the fact that she was silenced at the most opportune moment, the essential moment."

"But Dr. Crothers thinks Blair did it." Forbes was unaware that he had used her name. "I'm supposed to have paid her for the job. Is that it?"

"Presumably."

"And Brenning is doing everything he can to hush it up." Forbes was silent for a long time. It seemed to Blair that his face aged during that prolonged period of silence. At length he asked, "What do you suggest we do, Potter?"

"Call in the police without delay."

"Not just yet," Forbes said quickly. "Not just yet. Only if we find there's no other way—"

Mr. Potter shrugged. "Then we'll do the best we can to get at the bottom of this and let the chips fall where they may."

"There's no choice now," Forbes said grimly. "It was one thing to face these intolerable rumors for myself, but when an innocent bystander is involved I'll fight with everything I've got." He turned to Blair. "Nothing is going to happen to you," he promised, "and some day I'll find a way to make up to you for this—"

"You can go into that later," Mr. Potter broke in. "I'm borrowing Blair for the rest of the day. Incidentally, did you hear of her *coup* yesterday?"

"I was away all—I—" Forbes sat staring at Mr. Potter. "Look here, something queer happened. It has just occurred to me that there's a definite connection with Miss Kenyon's murder. I got a telephone call early in the morning telling me to go to Litchfield and wait at the inn for someone who could tell me who killed Connie and Evelyn. I went up there and waited for hours. Then I got a second message. I was given directions to go off on a side road, told to wait, that it might take a long time. Well, I waited until nearly five this morning before I decided it was a cruel hoax." He added with a short laugh, "It's not much of an alibi."

"Perhaps," Mr. Potter suggested thoughtfully, "it wasn't meant to be. Could you recognize the voice?"

Forbes shook his head. "It was muffled, almost a whisper."

"How did you get there?"

"I hired a taxi to and from Litchfield. I walked to the side road."

"Anyone see you?"

"At the inn, yes. Not at the place where I was told to wait. Only summer houses and they hadn't been opened for the season."

"And you were there how many hours—nearly eighteen? And no food?"

"I know how it sounds," Forbes agreed. "But you see I didn't dare take a chance on leaving. I thought whoever it was had had an accident or something and would come later. And I had to know."

There was small comfort in Mr. Potter's comment. "As you say, it's not much of an alibi." He turned to Blair. "Ready?"

She followed him out to the convertible. Mr. Potter shot her a speculative glance but she asked no questions until the car had gone through the covered bridge.

"Where are you taking me?"

"I want you to look through Miss Kenyon's house and her belongings. Do you mind?"

Blair set her teeth. "No, I don't mind." Her voice was stifled. "The only thing is that I spent just two nights there and scarcely was in the house at all. I shouldn't know if anything was missing or—wrong."

The house had a curious listening quality when Mr. Potter had unlocked the door and they went in. They stood in the living room for a moment, half expecting to hear a voice or a footstep but there was only the hum of the electric refrigerator and the drip of water leaking from the kitchen faucet.

Mr. Potter went into the kitchen and then into Blair's bedroom. He spent a few minutes checking the medicine chest. Then he went on to Miss Kenyon's room. After a few minutes he called Blair. She hesitated.

"It's all right," he said, "she isn't—they have taken her away."

The body was gone but the bed was still unmade, the pillow still dented by the hollow her head had made. Her underclothes were scattered untidily over the floor and a chair.

Mr. Potter watched as Blair's eyes moved slowly around the room. "Anything strike you as wrong—different?"

"The glass I heard her set down. Where is it?"

"Dr. Crothers took it with him. He turned it over to me this morning. Right now it is on its way to New York to be analyzed. Anything else?"

She shook her head. At Mr. Potter's suggestion she reluctantly went through the dresser drawers and the clothes closet, but found nothing that seemed wrong. Before the window there was a flat-topped desk that held an uncovered typewriter, an ashtray, a dictionary with a broken spine, and a stack of yellow paper.

Mr. Potter riffled through it and opened a drawer from which papers spilled. "Receipted bills, insurance policies, notes for books," he reported. "No letters. No snapshots."

"Tell me," Blair said, "what you hope to find. Something to prove Mr. Forbes is a murderer?"

"Something to indicate how much Miss Kenyon knew about the murders, some clue as to who brought her here."

"Why do you think she was killed?"

He sat back on his heels. "Well, if Forbes didn't do it, and I'm proceeding on the theory that he didn't, though I confess my mind is open on the subject, she was killed to prevent her from revealing the identity of the person who persuaded her to come here."

"But why would it matter enough, be important enough to kill her?"

"Because," he explained, "only one person would have a motive for bringing her here. Stop to think about it. What is Miss Kenyon's specialty? She writes books about men who have murdered their wives. Someone is fostering the idea that Forbes killed his wives. The arrival of Miss Kenyon, to gather material for a book, focuses a spotlight on Forbes. And only one person would find it necessary to do that—the person who wants Forbes convicted of murder. And then Miss Kenyon turns out to be an alcoholic and consequently unreliable. If she talks—"

"But she didn't know who it was until—I see, it's someone who was at the Brennings' and said something that betrayed himself to her. Someone," Blair caught her breath, "someone who was here in the night and accidentally flashed that light in my eyes. So we've got to find out where each of them was at that time."

"If we can," Mr. Potter reminded her. "Of course, as I am getting tired of insisting, the police could do it better and faster, but my hands are tied. Brenning is afraid of the police." He added more slowly, "So is Forbes."

When they were outside, he saw her draw a long breath of relief. "We'll drive somewhere and have a first-rate lunch," he said briskly, "then I'll take you back to the Brennings' to collect your things and deliver you to Mrs. Cook. Think you'll be comfortable there?"

"I'll like it. She's such a darling."

"How about meals?"

"I don't know. In any case, I'm dining with Charlie Forbes tonight."

Mr. Potter was thoughtful. "Charlie," he commented, "seems to be making quite a play for you."

"You know," Blair said unexpectedly, "I don't think he is. I have a curious feeling that he's simply trying to annoy his cousin."

"You are aware that he's a careless driver?"

"I have reason to be aware of it," Blair reminded him.

"Well, so long as you keep alert—do you own a revolver?"

"Good heavens, no! And I don't want one."

"Then take this." Mr. Potter groped in his vest pocket and pulled out a police whistle. "A cop who was a friend of mine gave me this. It's a good thing to have—just in case."

Blair dropped it into the deep pocket of her coat. "Thank you, I'll feel better having it. Just the same," she added confidently, "it isn't Charlie."

II

Joan, Mrs. Brenning explained to Mr. Potter, while Blair packed her suitcases, was taking a nap. She brightened a trifle when Mr. Potter suggested that Joan might like to dine with him and take in a movie, as it was too early for the summer theaters. But when Blair came down the stairs the older woman's face was stiff and she acknowledged the girl's thanks coldly.

Blair was flushed as she got into the yellow convertible. "Anyone would think," she said bitterly to Mr. Potter, "that woman actually believes she has been harboring a murderer."

"The Brennings don't actually think that. They're just uncertain and frightened. Badly frightened."

"I understand now how Mr. Forbes felt," Blair said. "To find yourself suspected of murder—it's so beastly and incredible."

As Mr. Potter turned into the gravel driveway at the Cooks', Emily ran down the steps to greet them.

"Come in, my dear! Welcome home. And Mr. Potter, too. Jerome is mixing drinks. You must join us."

Her welcome reached them like the touch of a friendly hand and she drew them into the house, talking volubly and eagerly. Only her troubled eyes, as she anxiously scanned Blair's pale face, betrayed how deeply worried she was.

Jerome Cook, in shirt sleeves, his arms moving rhythmically as he shook the cocktails, bald head gleaming from his exertion, beamed at them.

"You poor child," Emily exclaimed, "what a horrible experience for you. I should have insisted in the first place on your staying here."

Jerome chuckled. "You girls hurry with your arrangements." He held the shaker to his ear. "These cocktails are ready to pour. I hope you like rum."

When his wife had led Blair upstairs he turned to Mr. Potter and the good-humored smile faded from his face.

"This is the devil of a thing," he said soberly. "I just got the story from Glen. He's about at the end of his rope. And, involving the girl this way—of course, we'll keep an eye on her from now on but—" He poured the cocktails and mopped his head. "Emily is devoted to Glen and under all her cheerfulness she is horribly upset. What in hell is going on here, Potter? I've known Glen for over ten years and no one is going to make me believe he killed that woman to keep her from writing her damned book."

As he heard the voices of the two women on the stairs he said quickly, "We'll forget it now. I don't want Emily to know how serious it is. I'm not going to have her worried. We'll have a talk later."

His worn expression changed to one of joviality as he handed Blair and Emily their glasses. "Now," he said to Blair, "let's hear how you talked Miss Randall out of her antiques. Emily says you were terrific."

"Later," Emily interrupted. "She can tell you at dinner. But now I've got to know what has been happening. People are talking and—"

"I'm sorry," Blair said, "I didn't know you were expecting me for dinner."

"Why of course you are to have your meals here," Emily said emphatically. "Who ever heard of such a thing? Sending you out to forage for yourself at a drugstore or one of those awful places with juke boxes."

"But in any case, tonight I'm going out to dinner with Charlie Forbes."

"Oh," Emily said flatly. She set down her cocktail glass, her kind face troubled, and turned in appeal to her husband. "Jerome?"

He patted her hand. "We can't expect to keep a pretty girl all to ourselves. Charlie is a lucky young man." He added, smiling at his wife, "And a very nice one."

"Oh, yes," Emily agreed quickly. "Charlie is terribly nice, and great fun." She turned to Mr. Potter. "Did you get hold of him this morning?"

"No," Mr. Potter said, "he was out when I called.

"Did you want him for something—important?"

"Emily, my dear," her husband expostulated, laughing, "you really mustn't cross-examine the man."

Mr. Potter smiled. "It's all right. No secret. Blair had just called me about Miss Kenyon and I thought he might be able to give her a hand, you know."

"You should have told me," Emily said indignantly. "That poor girl, and a stranger here, too. I'd have gone for her at once."

Jerome had grasped the implication his wife had failed to see. "Charlie wasn't home? Well," he added comfortably, "he lives alone and doesn't like it. You

can't blame him for staying there as little as he can."
He frowned. "But it's curious, just the same."

"What's curious?" Emily asked.

"Well, if it should turn out to be another case like
Sarah, you know." Jerome explained to Mr. Potter.
"When you drove up I was just telling Emily about it.
Yesterday I got a call from my sister Sarah who lives in
Stamford. She's a professional invalid, poor soul, because she hasn't anything else to do, so she enjoys bad
health. Every now and then when she is bored she
thinks her last nour has come and she puts in a hurry
call for me. I went down, of course. Usually, I find her
lying on the couch, looking very pale and wan. This
time I found her busy cleaning house and very annoyed
at being caught at it. She hadn't sent for me. I stayed
on to pay her a visit because I hadn't seen her since
the first of the year but—I was wondering who did call
me and why. Queer business."

"Very queer," Mr. Potter admitted.

The front door banged open, there were rapid footsteps in the hall and Charlie Forbes came in, kissed
Emily, shook hands with the two men, and turned
smiling to Blair.

"What a time I had finding you!"

"Oh," she said in chagrin, "I forgot to let you
know."

"Well, after battering on the door of the cottage
loud enough to wake the dead—" he broke off with a
gasp. "Sorry. I went to the Center. Thought you might
be working overtime. Glen told me you were here. He
also told me about Miss Kenyon." Charlie was still
smiling but his expression was strained. "You found
her, didn't you?"

Blair shivered. "Yes, I found her."

"Well," Charlie said, *"de mortuis* and all that but
she wasn't a lovable character."

"Perhaps not," Blair agreed, "but somehow I felt
sorry for her. She was so frightened. And she had reason to be. She told me—"

"Suppose," Mr. Potter intervened quickly, "we try to forget about Miss Kenyon tonight. Blair has had enough of it for one day."

Charlie agreed. "Ready?" he asked. "I thought we might drive up to the Berkshire for dinner."

"I'll have to change. It will take only a few minutes."

When the girl had gone Jerome said, "Try to keep her mind off this thing tonight, Charlie. She's keyed up and under a strain."

"I'll keep her mind on me," Charlie said lightly. "If I can."

"Charlie," the irrepressible Emily broke in, "Mr. Potter tried to reach you this morning. He thought you might be of service to Blair but he couldn't find you."

Charlie's eyes were bright and wary. "I'm sorry about that. I'd have been glad to help in any way I could." He ignored the question in three pairs of eyes. "Are those cocktails for decoration or do I rate one?"

"Do you think," Emily said hesitantly, "if you are going to drive you ought to drink?"

"Suppose," Charlie said pleasantly, "you mind your own business, Emily, and let me handle my own." He poured a cocktail, drank it in three gulps and set down the glass. As Blair ran down the stairs in a lemon-colored dress he turned to look at her. "Well," he said slowly, "I ought to have a Rolls to do you justice."

Mr. Potter watched as the two went out of the house. He saw Jerome take Emily's groping hand in a comforting clasp.

"Won't you stay for dinner?" Emily asked as he turned to go. "I'd planned such a nice meal for Blair."

"Thanks, but I'm taking Joan Brenning out tonight."

"You are a really nice house guest, aren't you?" Emily smiled. "Squiring Joan around. Her mother will be so pleased to know she's with a suitable man. Why is it, I wonder, that girls are invariably attracted to the unsuitable ones? Sometimes I think falling in love is a temporary insanity."

"But pleasant," Jerome said with a laugh.

"Not really. It's too feverish. And the price is apt to come too high. But we're keeping Mr. Potter. You wouldn't care to bring Joan here, would you? Such a nice dinner, it's a shame to waste it."

"You are very kind," Mr. Potter told her, "but we had planned to dine at the Berkshire."

15

"So you see," Blair concluded, "Dr. Crothers thinks I killed her."

"I've always thought he couldn't tell a pregnancy from a broken arm, but this marks him out as incompetent if his whole career hadn't done it," Charlie said. "Anyone who could talk to you for five minutes or look at you for five seconds—" He shook his head in bewilderment. "At least, he won't dare open his mouth. Brenning has him muzzled. I never thought I would live to see the day when I'd be grateful to Brenning for anything."

He raised his hand to attract the waiter and ordered B & B with the coffee.

Blair, conscious that the two cocktails she had had before dinner, in addition to one with the Cooks, plus burgundy with the meal, had already loosened her tongue, refused. When they had started out, she had had no intention of discussing either the murder or her own incredible involvement in it, but the unaccustomed alcohol, abetted by Charlie's relaxed and friendly charm, had led her on, bit by bit, until she had poured out the whole story. Although she had an uneasy impression that Mr. Potter would not approve of her confidence, that he had doubts about her escort, she felt better for having talked out the problem.

Charlie, who had appeared to be irresponsible, proved on better acquaintance to be understanding and kind. From the moment when they had left the Cooks' house he had revealed unexpected qualities. His gaiety was tempered with gentleness, he had driven with exaggerated care which was, in itself, a tacit apology for the past and an earnest of reform for the future. He had paid her preposterous compliments with an undertone of seriousness, he had made her laugh, and finally he had persuaded her to talk. Blair found herself enjoying the evening to the hilt. And yet always she had a curious sensation of being not with Charlie but with Glen, a light-hearted Glen.

The impression was so strong that she was aghast to hear herself express it aloud. "You know, I have the strangest feeling that I am really dining with two men, you and your cousin. I suppose it's because you are so much alike."

The brightness faded from his face, intensifying the resemblance to Glen. "Oh," he said flatly, "that's rather—complicating." He turned the brandy glass around and around and finally set it on the table, pushed it away from him, untasted.

"Have I said something untactful?" Blair asked. "I didn't mean to. I've been having such a wonderful time."

He smiled and his face lighted up again. "Have you? I'm glad. So have I. It would be too bad if I were having all the fun. But of course I have an enormous advantage. I can look at you." He grinned wryly. "Blast it, you've curbed me. How can I tell you how pretty you are when there's a ghostly third with us?"

Blair laughed. "I only meant that there is such an extraordinary likeness, particularly when you both smile—though he doesn't smile so much."

Charlie gave her a quick glance and his own smile faded. "Glen," he said at last, "is a nicer guy than you've had a chance to find out. A series of bad breaks played hell with him, made him draw into himself too much." He added carefully, "Made him a little—suspicious. Not that he can be blamed for it. He—usually—gives everyone more than a fair break himself." Charlie forced a smile. "Take me, for example."

For a moment his eyes laughed at her, though there was still that disturbing undercurrent of seriousness.

"Yes, take me. I wish you would."

Blair laughed. "A shade premature, perhaps?"

"Who ever loved that loved not at first sight? Anyhow, I've put in my claim. That should give me a priority when you take the matter under advisement."

"I'll make a note of it," she promised.

"And lo, Ben Adhem's name led all the rest! Who could ask for anything more? But what were we—oh, yes, of course. I was talking about myself. Entrancing subject. And Glen. He has been more than a cousin. An older brother. Educated me, looked after me, gave me an income, got me out of scrapes. Ever since I was twelve and he was seventeen. It's a big debt, isn't it? Sometimes practically crushing. So when, occasionally, he gets off the beam, it's not too serious."

"I've found him very pleasant," Blair said and was aware of how stilted her words sounded even before she felt Charlie's eyes searching her face. She added hastily, "And your cousin Emily—"

"Oh, yes, Emily," Charlie grinned. "They broke the mold after they made Emily. I've never thought Jerome was quite up to her mark but they're as happy a couple as I've ever known. Emily had the money, of course, but she didn't care and neither did he. Started out to be an architect during the depression and got nowhere fast. He putters happily around the house and never seems to be bored. Emily adores him madly for reasons that escape me. He gives me the impression of being on the stodgy side. But I suppose no one understands the attractions between other people. Take Glen—well, no, perhaps you'd better not take Glen."

Once more Blair found Charlie watching her face intently. He laughed. "Shall we see what we can find in the way of a movie? At least we can give your lifeguard a short vacation."

"What on earth do you mean?"

"Potter. Hadn't you noticed? He and Joan Brenning are strategically seated across the room. No, up the other way. They haven't had dessert yet and Joan loves dessert. Shall we leave now and frustrate her?"

II

"They are leaving now," Joan said. "Do you want to follow them?"

"Follow them?" Mr. Potter echoed in a tone of surprise. "Of course not."

"Good. Then I can order crêpe suzette. Only I thought, as long as you'd followed them this far—"

"Sheer accident," Mr. Potter assured her. "This happens to be the best restaurant within reasonable driving distance. No wonder we both hit on it." He wished again that Charlie had selected a place with brighter lights. The flickering candles made it difficult for him to see Joan's eyes clearly.

He ordered crêpes suzette and while the waiter rolled a table beside them and busied himself with the chafing dish, they talked idly. But when the flaming liquid had been spooned over the crêpes and the rolled pastry had been lifted tenderly onto their plates, Joan reverted to the couple she had already left.

"The Masters girl really has something," she admitted, "those oriental eyes of hers and the way she does her hair, and I will say she knows how to wear her clothes. But," she added tartly, "if she thinks Charlie is serious she is wasting her time and someone ought to tell her. He just plays around. Always has. Always will. Somehow I can't picture him as Benedict the married man."

"I'm not so sure," Mr. Potter commented. "He seemed disturbed to think that I was being set up as his rival for you."

Joan started to speak, changed her mind. "Hiram, what really happened to the Kenyon woman? I said something at home about her being killed and Dad nearly snapped my head off. He's in a perfectly hellish temper tonight, anyhow. And mother has been trailing around after me all day, hinting and prying and whimpering. She's got a nasty suspicion about—"

"About Mr. Owen from Baltimore," Mr. Potter suggested.

"So it was a relief to get out of the house." Joan finished the dessert and scraped the plate with a spoon like a greedy child. "Does she have any money?"

Mr. Potter was taken aback. "Who?"

"The Masters girl, of course."

"Oh, no, nothing but her salary, I understand."

Joan looked more cheerful. "I was just wondering. Have you finished? Then let's go somewhere and do something. I hate just sitting around." She got impatiently to her feet before either Mr. Potter or the waiter could reach her chair.

In the lobby Mr. Potter brought her coat and put it over her shoulders. As she turned toward the door her face was brightly illuminated by a big chandelier. Abruptly he took her chin, tilted her head back, looked straight into her eyes. When he released her his face was grave.

III

"Jerome," Emily said. "Jerome!"

He turned from adjusting the radio dial, saw her expression and lowered the volume.

"You're worried about something," he said gently. "What is it?"

"Worried! I'm nearly frantic. Jerome, do you think it's all right?"

"What?"

"Blair going out with Charlie."

"Of course, it's all right. She's a charming girl and it's natural he would want—oh, you mean because of his driving? That accident the other night."

"No, he'll be careful," Emily said. "From now on I'm sure he'll be careful. But—"

There was the shadow of a smile around Jerome's lips. "Let's take a look at the awful thought."

Emily smiled ruefully. "Well, I was beginning to

think that Charlie was interested in Joan Brenning. He's hung around her a lot. And Blair is too nice a girl just for a second string."

"I expect Blair can handle the situation. After all, dinner and a movie hardly constitute a declaration of intentions."

"Oh, I know, but just the same—and, anyhow," she went on a trifle incoherently, "what will Glen do when he knows Charlie is paying attention to Blair, too?"

"Blair, too?"

"Well—Connie and then Evelyn. Somehow, I got the impression that Glen likes Blair a lot."

"She's a very attractive girl."

"He seems—oh, aware of her, even when he isn't looking at her or speaking to her. And Blair likes him, too. Miss Randall spotted it right away. She told Blair flat out that she was head over heels in love with him."

"Sounds like you," Jerome was amused. He pulled his wife to her feet and put his arm around her. "How about worrying over your own man for a change? What are we having for dinner?" He led her toward the kitchen. She stopped and turned to put her hands on his shoulders.

"You're shaking!" he exclaimed. "Look here, my dearest, fond as I am of both the Forbes men, neither of them is worth having you worried."

"Worried," his wife wailed. "Oh, Jerome, I hope I'm just being a fool but I'm frightened. I'm frightened!"

IV

"I'm frightened."

In spite of his perturbation, Brenning felt himself expand in response to his wife's confession. Never before had Beulah, the dominant, the assured, appealed to his superior strength. His voice dropped at least two tones, acquired a new resonance.

"Don't be absurd, Beulah. There's absolutely no reason to be frightened. Joan is just young and high spirited."

"You talk as though she were a prancing horse," his wife declared, and burst into tears.

As she was perfectly capable of carrying her point by sheer persistence she had never needed to fall back on tears. Brenning got out of his chair and went to pat her helplessly on the head, mussing her wave.

She jerked away from him. "And you p-pat me as though I were a pet dog," she said hysterically.

Standing over her he felt at an advantage. He took her arms in his hands. "Stop it, Beulah."

His air of authority had so often been pure bluster that she was surprised by his assurance. She gulped down a sob and blew her nose.

"Now, then, let's talk about it quietly."

"How can I be quiet when I'm discussing my only child?"

"Mine, too, unless you've been deceiving me all these years. What's wrong with Joan?"

"Stanley, she—she was with a man in New York. There was something about her when she came home—I couldn't mistake it."

"Joan?" he said incredulously. "Joan!"

She nodded.

The temporary assurance was gone. Brenning collapsed on the edge of a chair. "You're sure? Not imagining things?"

"I'm not imagining it. Anyhow, she—she hardly seems to care whether I know or not."

"God!" he whispered to himself. After a moment he asked, "Who's the man? Potter?"

"Hiram! Of course not. I don't know who it is, Stanley, and I've gone crazy trying to figure it out."

He flung out his hands in a gesture of defeat. The shoulders he had been holding so squarely, slumped.

"But why, Beulah? Why would she do that? If she's in love, if she wants to get married, we wouldn't stand in her way."

Mrs. Brenning heard the note of broken appeal and for the first time in years drew his head down, kissed him spontaneously. They clung to each other, ship-wrecked.

"I've thought and thought," she said. "Joan wanted Paul Brooks to come to dinner. She insisted."

"But Brooks is old enough to be her father!"

"Well, sometimes girls find older men more interesting. Or it might be Charlie, of course."

"I'd kill him before I'd let him marry her," Brenning said, his face mottled with rage.

"You see? Maybe Joan knew that."

"We'll have it out with her tomorrow. That's all we can do." Brenning dropped into a chair, his hands kneading the back of his neck.

"One of your bad headaches?"

He nodded. "Everything seems to go wrong at once. I must be getting old. I don't know how to cope with things."

"It's my fault," she said with her new humility. "I shouldn't have asked Hiram Potter up here. Everything was all right until he came. Then Miss Kenyon was killed."

"Died of a heart attack," he reminded her automatically.

"Died of a heart attack," she repeated. "But who really killed her, Stanley? Was it Glen to stop her book? Was it?"

"Glen is my client," Brenning said. "My clients are always innocent."

"You know," his wife remarked in a tone of profound surprise, "Hiram really believes Glen may be innocent."

"Then he'd be wise to stop interfering. Between them, he and Glen are doing their best to put Glen in the electric chair. The whole town is talking more openly than before, more hostile in manner. And, of course, Brooks is cashing in on it. And on top of everything else, George Harrison has been stealing money from Glen who wants to prosecute. He can't stand a suit right now. Get Harrison in a witness chair and he might turn nasty. Very nasty indeed."

"That horrid little man couldn't hurt Glen."

"Hurt him," Brenning exclaimed. "He could destroy him."

16

"And," in her excitement Blair picked up the list and flourished it over her head, "so help me, there's a sleigh bed built in the early 1800s that women will drool over and a Hepplewhite field bed, late 1700s, that is in perfect condition. When word gets out, there will be a traffic jam all the way from Hawthorne Circle as people start flocking up here. This place is going on the map. There will be news stories about it, I shouldn't wonder. Guide books will list it—with stars. Why—"

Glen Forbes whose manner had been restrained to the point of coolness when she had arrived that morning, leaned against the wall of the barn and laughed aloud. His eyes were alight. He was as gay as Charlie. Blair found herself laughing with him.

"I know I'm ridiculous," she admitted shamelessly, "but it's such a wonderful thing to have happen to the Center. And now of all times!"

"What magic did you use on Miss Randall?" he asked curiously. "You know, you have potentialities I didn't expect. I'd never have dreamed of tackling her. Antique dealers have been known to commit hari-kari on her doorstep and she didn't turn a hair."

"I just told her what you were trying to accomplish here. That's what really won her."

"That—and you."

He did not move a step toward her but all at once Blair felt that he was too close.

"Well," she said, a trifle out of breath, "we'd better start getting this place in order so that there will be room to display some of the Randall pieces to the best advantage."

The laughter in his eyes made her race on, "Only a few pieces at a time, of course. Anyhow, we'll want some lower priced stuff for the regular road trade. Tourist bait." She bent over and busily pushed a packing box out of the way.

His voice was grave but there were lines of amusement around his lips when he said, "There's not such a terrible rush as all that, you know." He picked up the box. "Where do you want it?"

"Well, I—" she looked around vaguely, saw his expression and blushed. "Oh, I don't blame you for laughing at me."

He set down the box. "I wasn't," he said. "Not really. I think I was just laughing because I was happy."

The sunlit doorway was darkened for a moment and then George Harrison came inside, looked from Blair to Forbes and back to Blair, his small beadlike eyes bright with malice.

"Morning, Miss Masters. I'm glad to see you looking so gay—alluring is the word—after your tragic experience yesterday. That poor woman. Died in her sleep, I've been told."

Blair nodded at him but did not speak.

"Morning, Glen. Where are the books? I can't find them."

"Yesterday I turned them over to a public accountant."

Blair bent over the box of hooked rugs and began to unpack it, shake the rugs out, spread them on the floor of the barn as far away from the two men as possible. Harrison had effectively destroyed her recent mood. And perhaps, she thought, it was just as well. Something about the Forbes men broke down her reserves to an alarming extent.

"You can't do it," Harrison said at last.

"I've already done it," Forbes assured him. "Look here, George, you brought this on yourself. If you'd shown any signs of wanting to make restitution, if you'd even had an excuse for taking the money—but instead of that you threatened me."

"You can't do it," Harrison repeated. His voice was shrill. "You can't send me to prison. You start anything like that and you'll wish you were dead. Good God, do you know what people are saying about you now? Put me on the stand and I'll give them something to talk about, something really juicy."

"Save it until then." Forbes' big vibrant voice held a warning which made Blair swing around in alarm to stare at him, but Harrison, frightened and angry, rushed on to his doom.

"Do you suppose I don't know why you married Evelyn? The big Forbes marrying drab little Evelyn? Well, I know, all right. Because Evelyn knew the truth about Connie and Charlie. Because—"

Forbes made a low sound in his throat and launched himself at Harrison. Blair pressed the back of her hand to her mouth as though to shut off a cry and watched in horror the red glint in Forbes' eyes, his terrible white face, the savage driving blows. He's going to beat him to death, she thought. He is deliberately beating him to death.

"Stop it, you fools!" Charlie yelled from the doorway and hurled himself at the two struggling men, pulling his cousin back with all his strength. Harrison scrambled to his feet, stumbled toward the door and ducked outside while the two Forbes men stood panting, glaring at each other.

"Are you crazy?" Charlie demanded at length. "You might have killed the guy. Aren't things bad enough without stirring up more trouble? You don't want George to go around shooting off his mouth, do you?"

Forbes freed the arm which Charlie was still clutching, straightened his tie and his hair. "Why not?" he said. "From now on I'm all in favor of things being said out loud. That way I can answer them. It might clear the atmosphere, which has become a trifle sticky. Or hadn't you noticed it?"

Charlie's mouth twitched in a nervous grimace but he made no answer.

"Or hadn't you noticed it, Charlie?" Glen's voice was almost gentle. "Did you hear George explain the reason for my second marriage? He claims I married Evelyn to shut her up because she knew too much about Connie's relations with—"

"Glen! Glen, for God's sake!" Charlie's tormented face left the other man unmoved. "If that's what you have been thinking—"

"I'm thinking that we can get on with our work here as soon as you clear out."

"That's why I came," Charlie said. "I thought I could help Blair get the place in order."

"Let Blair alone, Charlie. Keep away from her."

"Oh, God," Charlie said in a half whisper and went out of the barn.

Blair dropped down on the packing box, her elbows on her knees, her head in her hands. And Forbes, his voice tired, said, "So that's that. It's been a good try but it won't work. Whatever I touch I poison. Don't look so frightened and sick at heart. None of us are worth it. I'll give up the Center. I was a fool to try it in the first place. Go away, Blair; go back to New York and sanity."

She stood up to face him, her clenched hands thrust deep into her pockets. "I'm not going. And I don't like people who give up and run away. Anyhow, you can't do it. You can run and run, but whatever you run from always keeps up with you. It's never vanquished until you stand and face it. I'm going to stay here and fight. And so are you. We haven't any real choice." She caught sight of his skinned hand. "But not that way."

"How then?" he asked quietly. "How?" And took her in his arms. He kissed her lightly, almost casually. Then his arms tightened, he pulled her against him and kissed her again, demandingly.

Blair, who had been rigid with surprise and protest, pushed against him. Then her mouth answered his, her arms crept around him.

At length he held her off so that he could look at her, at the dark shining cap of hair, the slanted smoky blue eyes, the flushed cheeks, the mouth still tremulous from his lips. He kissed it again.

"This was bound to happen from the moment you walked into my office," he told her. "I knew it then. Didn't you?"

Blair looked at him and they exchanged a delighted smile.

And from the doorway Paul Brooks laughed aloud.

II

Lunch with the Cooks was a cheerful meal in a sunny room. Afterwards Blair, still in a happy daze, stopped at a hardware store for a hammer and nails and a couple of big lamps for the barn. This afternoon she and Glen would start work getting the place in order.

Her rose-tinted mood lasted until she reached the street and waited for the clerk to put her purchases in the station wagon. Even when the chant first began she did not understand. She listened to it, half smiling, until the words penetrated, the smile froze on her lips.

"Sister Ann, Sister Ann, do you see anyone coming?"

Three or four high-school girls were laughing, chanting, staring at her. Then, made uneasy by her fixed white face, they ran off down the street, giggling.

Blair started the car, numb with shock. People didn't do things like that. She drove slowly back to the Center. It was very quiet. All the workmen had gone. Their trucks and tools had been taken away. She parked the car on the silent green and went up to the door of the barn. Its fresh white paint was scarred by a word splashed across it in red paint: Bluebeard.

She unlocked the door with a shaking hand and went inside. Slowly she took off her coat, pushed back her hair, looked around dumbly. She should get started at something but the exhilaration was gone. Nothing was left but unspeakable ugliness. She bent over to pick up the hooked rugs she had left on the floor when the fight began between Glen and Harrison. As she did so there was a crash, a thud, a tinkle of broken glass.

She heard a shout and the sound of running feet and reached for the stone that had so nearly struck her.

The door was flung open and Glen ran in. "Are you hurt?"

She shook her head, wordlessly handed him the stone.

"It was a kid, just a kid," he said in a tone of incredulity. "I saw him start to throw it as I was coming out of the office."

"Did you see the door?"

He nodded. "And the workmen all quit without notice. I guess we are in for something pretty bad, Blair. It's got out of control."

He reached for the telephone and called Brenning, first at his office, then at his house. He talked briefly. "And bring Potter," he concluded.

He put down the telephone and saw her folding the rugs. "Let them go, for God's sake," he said irritably. "This changes everything. Can't you see that?"

She looked at him blankly, at a loss to know how to meet this new mood of his.

He laughed harshly. "Everything is changed, I said. That little episode before lunch—forget it. Even savages, who appear to have some strange mating customs, don't woo a woman by stoning her. Or expecting her to succeed two murdered women. It's over. It's done."

Within fifteen minutes the two men arrived in Mr. Potter's convertible. When they came in, Brenning was stuttering with rage.

"Who wrote that word on the door? You've got to clean it off at once. You can't leave it there."

"And a rock through the window," Mr. Potter said. "You're right, Forbes, there's no more time to waste. Let's get down to it."

Brenning hesitated, looking at Blair.

"Blair is in this because we got her into it," Mr. Potter said.

"But—"

"Blair stays," Forbes said. "We'll move over to the office where we can sit down."

When they were settled, Brenning said, "What happened to start this violence? I've been afraid of this. The town is in an ugly mood. But I thought if we kept the Kenyon death quiet—what happened this morning?"

Forbes smiled faintly. "Practically everything. I beat hell out of Harrison, quarreled with Charlie, and told Brooks I'd break him in two."

Brenning moaned. "Sometimes I think you are as irresponsible as Charlie. This is no time to be making enemies."

Forbes gave a short bark of laughter.

"All right," Brenning agreed, "I'll admit that one of them must be behind this sabotage. My own guess would be Harrison. He's mean and vindictive and vengeful. Just the same, Glen, my advice to you is not to prosecute. He can do you a lot of harm."

"Do you really believe that, Stan?" Forbes asked curiously.

"Understand," Brenning said, flustered, "I don't say Harrison is telling the truth but—"

"I'm going to prosecute."

"Why do you hire a lawyer if you won't take his advice? You go on as you damned please, regardless of my opinion. I tell you for the last time, you're leading with your chin if you tangle with Harrison. And another thing, you are still intestate. For a man with your holdings that is criminal stupidity. If anything were to happen to you now—"

Forbes laughed, scribbled a few words on a piece of paper, folded it and handed it to the lawyer. "You can draw up a new will today, if it will make you any happier. Those are my wishes."

Brenning opened the paper and his face turned purple with anger. "That's preposterous. This is no joke. It's serious business."

"I'm perfectly serious."

"Suppose," Mr. Potter broke in, "we stick to the main issue for awhile. The main issue, as you tend to forget, is that three women have been murdered: Constance Forbes, Evelyn Forbes, Ann Kenyon. Those women died by violence. So far as Glen's wives are concerned, whatever clues there may have been are gone now, destroyed long ago.

"But Ann Kenyon died only yesterday. There are things to be discovered. For instance, what put her on to the Bridgetown murders in the first place? Who obtained those sleeping pills? Those are jobs—this is all a job—for the highly qualified men in the police force. I urge you now, Forbes, to call them in without another hour's delay, and put the whole problem squarely in their hands."

"No," Brenning exploded, hitting the desk with his clenched fist. "Glen wouldn't stand a chance. As you say, there's no evidence to be unearthed at this late date on the deaths of Connie and Evelyn but, by God, there's public opinion. So far as Miss Kenyon is concerned, Dr. Crothers would testify, if he was pushed far enough, that Blair Masters was the most likely person to have killed her, and that she is employed by Glen. We can't do that!"

Mr. Potter shrugged his shoulders. "We'll let it go for the moment but we'll have to come back to it. The police are not anxious to send an innocent man to the chair and they are anxious to stop a killer. They also know their jobs. However—"

He smiled suddenly. "Let's start with the worst possibility and see what we can do with it. The biggest puzzle is: Why were those three women murdered? The obvious person is Forbes himself."

"Naturally," Forbes agreed. "That sticks out a mile."

"Of course," Mr. Potter went on, "you may be a

compulsive killer. If we have to, we'll put you under observation. Personally, I think you're sane enough. But supposing that you are Miss Kenyon's killer—why are you?"

Forbes watched him without a word.

"Your first wife, Connie, was an attractive girl, an old friend. I gather you drifted into marriage with her somewhat casually. Sorry if I'm being offensive."

"Damnably offensive," Forbes agreed. "Still, I suppose you can't help it."

"When she died the only person to benefit by her death was Paul Brooks. So, financially, you gained nothing. On the other hand, if the marriage was an unhappy one—"

His words hung in air for a moment. "Echo answers nothing," he said at last.

"If it had been unhappy," Brenning pointed out impatiently, "there are divorce courts. As a matter of fact, it was a very happy marriage. Glen and Connie were a devoted couple."

Forbes said nothing at all.

"But if there had been any bitterness," Mr. Potter persisted, "if Forbes, for instance, had believed his wife to be unfaithful—"

"Where did you pick up that filth?" Brenning snapped.

"From your daughter Joan."

Brenning was silenced.

"So you see that financial profit isn't the only possibility. Then we come to Forbes' second wife, Evelyn."

"I suppose," Brenning snorted, "you've heard that she was unfaithful, too."

"It has been suggested. And by the way," Mr. Potter held up his hand to check the irate lawyer, "I understand that you are the source of that particular rumor. Eye witness, or something of the sort."

This time Forbes stirred, cast a hard look at Brenning.

The lawyer mopped his head. "You understand how

it is, Glen. I thought I saw—I might have been mistaken—"

Then Forbes spoke. "There's another possibility, Potter. Harrison suggested it this morning. I married his cousin Evelyn because she knew I had killed Connie and wanted to buy her silence. Then, getting weary of my bargain, I ran her down."

Mr. Potter listened without comment. "And now we come to the third murder—Miss Kenyon's. There, of course, you have the only obvious motive, Forbes. You killed her to prevent her from exposing you by writing her book. And, most unfortunately, you have no alibi for the time when the sleeping pills must have been administered."

Forbes stretched out his hands. "I seem to hear the clanking of gyves. Are you going to turn me in now? Naturally, I'm guilty."

"No hurry," Mr. Potter said mildly. "We've got to clear off the other possibilities first."

"Do you mean Brooks or Harrison?"

"Well, neither one. I think I'd start with Jerome Cook."

17

"Oh, really," Brenning said in a tone of exasperation, "must we go in for fooling? I'd as soon suspect Emily or my own wife."

"And yet," Mr. Potter said, "there and only there do we find the most common of all motives for murder: profit. Let's suppose that Jerome Cook wants money, a lot of money, Forbes' money."

"I won't suppose anything of the kind," Brenning snorted. "In the first place, you seem to overlook the fact that Emily inherited as much as Glen."

"But where is it?" Mr. Potter asked gently. "There are no indications of wealth in the Cook household. Jerome toils not, neither does he spin. Suppose, having gone through his wife's money, he wants his brother-in-law's as well. What stood in the way? Connie. So he—eliminated her. After her death to whom did you leave your money, Forbes?"

"To Emily," Forbes said stiffly.

Mr. Potter nodded. "But then you married again and there was a new beneficiary. So Jerome decided on more sweeping measures. He kills Evelyn in the same way, under the same conditions. Why? Obviously, to shout foul play at the top of his voice. A gigantic gamble to get rid of your beneficiary and you at the same time, you who, as he knew, had actually run down a man and killed him years before.

"But he miscalculated. You were born in Bridgetown and the people saw you grow up, liked and trusted you. Not only were you not accused of killing your wives but you did the unexpected thing. Emily was no longer your beneficiary. Instead, you tied up everything you had in the Center for the benefit of the community. So the plans had to change. You must be eliminated, but in such a way that the Center won't get the money.

"Paul Brooks wanted the land and he wasn't a man to pass up any weapon, however dirty it might be, that fell into his hands. It is suggested to him that the Center is your bribe to the town for immunity in regard to the murders of your wives. Brooks jumps at it. He may even have believed it. It is so easy to believe what we want to believe. Rumors begin to spread. But you still have friends and an almost impregnable position."

Mr. Potter lighted a cigarette. "I'll go on supposing. Jerome, looking around for something to crystallize the case against you, comes across one of Ann Kenyon's books and he gets an idea. If the writer on modern Bluebeards were to come to Bridgetown for a subject, no one could escape that pointing finger. You'd be in a hell of a spot. The town would have to take steps, would refuse your bribe; you'd be convicted of murder, and Emily, as next of kin, would inherit."

Watching Mr. Potter, Blair was puzzled. What on earth was he trying to do? For he knew, as she did, that Jerome Cook had been with his sister in Stamford when Miss Kenyon took the sleeping pills. Uneasily, she felt that the slim, fair-haired man with the bland face was skillfully playing on Forbes. She tried to catch his eyes, seeking for the comfort of a glance that would tell her they were partners in this, but Forbes appeared to have forgotten her existence, wholly concentrated on what Mr. Potter was saying.

"Tomfoolery," Brenning said shortly. "Jerome doesn't care a hang about money. Better for them both if he did."

"What happened to Emily's inheritance?"

"Some ill-judged investments. Nothing criminal." There was a sneer in the lawyer's voice.

"Then," Mr. Potter went on, speaking a little faster,

"if you don't like my case against Jerome, we come to Charlie Forbes."

Forbes spoke now. "That's out, Potter. There has never been any question of making Charlie my heir. He knows that. He has an income, enough to keep him modestly. That's all. It's all he will ever have from me."

"But not everyone looks for the big scoop," Mr. Potter reminded him. "Charlie, if I have summed him up correctly, is what my aunt calls 'bone lazy.' To lose an income, even a small one, that would enable him to live without working, would be a catastrophe for him. And he might well lose it."

His voice grew more incisive. "Only a fool could be unaware of the hostility, the distrust between you and your cousin. And there are rumors everywhere that he was—to put it bluntly—intimate with both your wives."

"That's a goddamned lie!"

Mr. Potter ignored Forbes' terrible white-hot anger. "And there is Charlie's growing reputation for being accident prone. Would you like to assure me that you are convinced he did not run down your wives, either accidentally or deliberately?"

Forbes was silent for a moment. Then he said grimly, "Go on, you are doing the talking."

No, Blair cried silently to herself. No, Glen. You can't do that. You are throwing Charlie to the wolves.

"And, of course," Mr. Potter went on, "there's Paul Brooks, who got three hundred thousand dollars by Connie's death. He wants the Center for his housing development and he wants you intestate. We know he has been assiduous in stirring up trouble for you, that he drove you to break your will."

Brenning looked more cheerful. "That's one point you can't miss," he declared. "Brooks is the only person who has actually gained anything. And that's without any idiotic supposing. That's a matter of record."

"So it is," Mr. Potter agreed amiably. "And, finally, we come to George Harrison. I don't believe for a mo-

ment that he killed those women but I do believe he
could tell us who is guilty. Because someone is stirring
up violence and as George has proved himself to be a
thief and a blackmailer he seems to me the logical man
to be doing the dirty work. He obviously expects to be
paid for it."

"So that's the lot," Brenning said, "and not a shred
of proof to back any of it. Actually, Hiram, what do
you really think?"

"First," Mr. Potter said, "I'm going to try to find out
where all four men were at the time when Miss Kenyon
took the sleeping pills. We'll be able to eliminate some
of them. Bound to. Only, I repeat, the police could do
it better and faster. I have a growing impression that
time is running out."

Brenning pushed back his chair. "Now, Forbes," he
said in the tone of a man trying to be reasonable,
"about this new will of yours—"

"You have my instructions."

Brenning shrugged his shoulders and reached for his
hat. "Coming, Hiram?"

Mr. Potter paused at the door, came back. "That violence this afternoon was only the beginning. Be careful, Forbes." He met the light eyes steadily. "Be very
careful."

II

As they drove away from the Center Mr. Potter said,
"Shall I leave you at your office?"

"Take me to the Cooks'," Brenning said. "Maybe
Emily can talk some sense into Glen. Know what he
has done now? Given me instructions for a new will,
leaving everything—but everything, even Charlie's al-
lowance—to the Masters girl."

"The utter fool," Mr. Potter groaned. He stopped
the car.

"What are you going to do?"

"I'm going back to the Center. It's not just that
Forbes is endangering Blair, he's putting a rope around

his neck as well as hers. I've got to stop him."

"Not now, Hiram. There's something I've got to discuss with you."

"More urgent than that?"

"More urgent to me," Brenning said grimly. "Who was the man with Joan the other night in New York? My wife is sure there was someone. If you know, in the name of heaven, tell me who it is."

"I don't know," Mr. Potter admitted, "but persuade Joan to tell you, if you can."

"She won't. She doesn't deny it. She just laughs. What has happened to the young, Hiram?"

"Usually they are what their parents and circumstances have made them. But keep at her. She may be glad to talk when she realizes that we are looking for alibis for that night."

Brenning swiveled around in surprise. "You think it's one of them?"

Mr. Potter explained how he had overheard her telephone conversation. "She made her plans at the dinner party," he said. "She was different after that."

At the Cooks' house he asked, "By the way, where would I be likely to find Paul Brooks at this time of day?"

"He has a real estate office in his house on the avenue. Old red brick place. Is he—?" Brenning looked at Mr. Potter with an anguished unspoken question and then went slowly up to the Cooks' front door, looking old and defeated.

There was a small ornamental sign on the neat lawn: Paul Brooks—Country Properties. A pimply faced clerk admitted Mr. Potter to a big square room whose beautifully proportioned lines delighted him. On the panels of a folding screen were fastened pictures and descriptions of country estates. While Mr. Potter looked them over, the clerk went in search of Paul Brooks.

He entered the room a few minutes later, looked in surprise at Mr. Potter and then came forward to shake hands, ruddy face smiling.

"This is an unexpected pleasure. Is your visit social or are you looking for a place in the country? I've got a couple of terrific bargains right now so you couldn't have chosen a better time. Slack season, you know."

"Actually," Mr. Potter said, "I have come here to be extremely impertinent. I'd like to know where you were Tuesday night."

The remark was so totally unexpected that Brooks required several seconds to grasp it. Even then he seemed unable to understand the purport of the question.

"Tuesday night?" His salesman's smile was still on his lips. Gradually it faded. "I'm flattered by this interest in my affairs, Mr. Potter, but I fail to see why you want to know."

"Actually," Mr. Potter said apologetically, "there's no reason why you should tell me. But I thought—that is, the general opinion seems to be, that it would be much pleasanter to keep all this from the police, you know. I mean, as long as we can, and as much as we can." He had never seemed more ineffectual, more helpless, and something in his air of abject apology amused Brooks.

He grinned. "What have the police got to do with the way I spent Tuesday night?"

"Nothing. That is, I sincerely hope not. The difficulty, you know," he lowered his voice, "the real difficulty is that Miss Kenyon was given a fatal dose of sleeping pills sometime Tuesday night."

Brooks gave a loud incoherent exclamation. His expression changed from surprise to a guarded alertness.

"We've been giving the matter a great deal of thought," Mr. Potter said earnestly, "and it's obvious she was killed by someone who heard her talk at the Brennings' dinner, realized she was a garrulous drunk. Someone who brought her to Bridgetown to constitute a living threat to Forbes. Because she had to be tipped off, you know. There was no publicity on the way the Forbes women died. So it struck us as a—a kind of preliminary clearing of the decks—to find where everyone was when she took those pills."

"It struck you that way, did it?" Brooks gave an angry laugh. "Have you inquired where Forbes was at the crucial time?"

"Oh, yes," Mr. Potter assured him. "And I'll check it most carefully. But I thought, if you could just tell me in confidence—you see, you keep intruding in Forbes' affairs in the most confusing way. All that public talk, which does put you on record, you know—most awkward. Running down the Center and Forbes' motives in creating and endowing it, when your own motives for wanting the land, you see—" Mr. Potter made a vague gesture. "So much to gain from a housing development. And Connie did leave you hundreds of thousands. Of course, you and I know how it is, but things like that do create a bad impression, don't they?"

Brooks swallowed his anger and his impatience with the younger man. Futile and confused as he obviously was, nevertheless he had a point.

"Well," he said, "if it's any comfort to you I wasn't in Bridgetown at all from mid-afternoon Tuesday until the next morning. Matter of fact, I never am. I have a kind of standing date in Hartford. It's been going on for years."

"I suppose," Mr. Potter suggested, "she will back you up on that."

"Oh, yes," Brooks said without hesitation, "she will back me up."

"Does anyone here know about this arrangement of yours?"

Brooks shrugged. "In a small community, people always know more about you than you realize."

"And where can the lady be reached?"

"How much publicity is this going to get?"

"None, if you are in the clear. I can give you my personal assurance on that."

Brooks looked him over. "I guess," he said slowly, "that's good enough. Her name is Mrs. Tennelson." He supplied the address in Hartford. "What got you into this, Potter? Curiosity?"

"I don't like murder," Mr. Potter said quietly. "And may I give you a word of warning, Mr. Brooks? Be rather guarded in any accusation you may make in the next few days. You could set off a charge of dynamite and there's no telling who might get hurt. And you really should safeguard your own interests, you know. Up to now you have let yourself be used to a criminal extent."

"Let myself be used! What in hell are you getting at?"

"Those stories you have been so assiduously circulating about Forbes. They aren't your own idea, are they? But if Forbes should decide to sue you for libel, you'd be the one to pay."

Mr. Potter added vaguely, "I should think a man would feel like an awful fool when he discovers he has been a cat's paw."

18

When he had left a thoughtful Brooks behind him, Mr. Potter climbed into the convertible. Today the sky was clear and the air had the light, tingling excitement of spring. He pressed a lever to let the top back and the sun fell warm on his sleek fair head. He made a mental note of Mrs. Tennelson. Obviously she would back Brooks' alibi. His confidence in naming her had made that clear. What was needed was someone adept at dealing with women of her kind. Another job for Sam Trumble, he decided.

His own immediate task was to find Charlie Forbes and he did so by the simple expedient of turning his head. Charlie was across the street, lounging outside the bank building, talking idly to a couple of men. Mr. Potter touched the horn and Charlie looked up, waved, and came across the street.

"If you aren't doing anything," Mr. Potter proposed, "and it's not too early for a drink, hop in and we'll see what we can find."

"I never do anything," Charlie assured him cheerfully, "and it's always time for a drink. There's a good place a couple of miles out of town. First-rate whisky and no juke box. Just go straight ahead. I'll direct you."

The whisky was all he claimed for it and the place was deserted except for an amorous couple in a booth near the back who had eyes only for each other.

"And what," Charlie asked pleasantly over a second scotch and water, "do you want for your drinks?"

"Information." Mr. Potter was disarmingly frank. "To be specific, an alibi. And, I hope to God, a nice clear-cut alibi with half a dozen witnesses."

Charlie's expression was guarded. "Sounds interesting. What for? Who for?"

"For Tuesday night when someone gave Ann Kenyon a glass of whisky loaded with sleeping pills."

Charlie drained his glass. "May I ask," he said politely, "whether this little interview is Glen's idea?"

"It is entirely my own idea. You see," Mr. Potter might have been discussing a brand of cigarettes, "one of you four men is a killer. I'm trying to eliminate as far as possible before the police come in."

Charlie's jaw tightened. "I see. Well, I haven't an alibi that's worth a damn. I got a telephone call Tuesday morning saying that if I'd go over to the inn at Sharon I'd be told how Connie and Evelyn were killed. I went and dangled my heels half the day in the inn. Then I got another call, sending me out on a deserted side road where I was told to wait because there might be delays and there would be no second chance. So I waited. I was there all night before I gave up."

His eyes met Mr. Potter's in a challenge that would have been more effective if he hadn't been so white. "A little stinker of an alibi, isn't it? Ever hear one like it?"

"Oh, yes," Mr. Potter said wearily, "your cousin Glen has one just like it, except that he went to Litchfield."

Charlie thought it over. "So we could both be lying, or one of us could have stacked the cards against the other, or we're supposed to cancel each other out."

"Those are all possibilities."

"Or someone went to a hell of a lot of trouble to put us both in a spot. For my money, it's Brooks. You had better check up on him, Potter."

"I'm going to do that now," Mr. Potter assured him. "I suppose you didn't recognize the telephone voice."

"No, it was disguised. Blurry. Makes it nice for me, doesn't it?"

Mr. Potter ignored the mocking comment. "By the way, do you know the name of Jerome Cook's sister and her address? She seems to be his alibi."

"Sobbing Sal? She's a widow, name's Fitch. Mrs. Ronald Fitch. Somewhere in Stamford is all I know. She comes up here occasionally, takes pills, moans, takes drops, sobs, trails back. Not a bit like jovial Jerome."

"Another drink?"

Charlie shook his head. "Look here, Potter, for what it's worth, I didn't kill the Kenyon woman. I don't know who did except that it couldn't have been Glen. And I know damned well it wasn't me, though someone seems to want to keep me from proving it."

"Someone," Mr. Potter said, "is getting desperate."

"For God's sake, you don't think anything else will happen?"

"It's bound to, you know. If you'll take a word of advice, stay quietly at home for awhile."

"What good do you expect that to do?"

"Well," Mr. Potter said vaguely, "you never can tell, can you?"

II

It was nearly ten o'clock when Sam Trumble tapped on the door of an apartment in Hartford. Laughing voices broke off and a woman's high heels tapped across the floor. She opened the door and looked inquiringly at him.

"Mrs. Tennelson?"

"That's right." She was a heavily built woman in her late thirties with dyed blond hair and smooth make-up. The kind of woman whom people call a good sport, cheerful, undemanding, eager to have a good time and supply a good time. Sam Trumble had seen carbon copies of her in dozens of bars. Mr. Brooks was not, perhaps, fastidious, but he could have done worse.

"I'm an insurance investigator. There was a little fire

here in the building on Tuesday and I'm wondering whether you could tell me—"

"Tuesday!" Her eyes met his in a question. Abruptly she stepped outside and closed the door. "What have you really come for?"

"Has Mr. Brooks been in touch with you?"

She nodded. "Look, it's just one of those things. He comes up here once a week. My friends think we're married. He's Tennelson here, a traveling salesman. It's not that I want to put anything over, but you know how women are. If they find you're not really married they get awfully moral about it because they are afraid for their own husbands. Think you are prowling. Okay?"

"Okay," Sam agreed with a grin.

She conducted him into the living room where a couple was sitting over a scrabble board, a tall angular man of forty with a small plump cheerful wife, who were introduced as the Williamses from across the hall.

"Joe is cheating," Mrs. Williams cried with the unaccustomed coyness induced by the presence of a male stranger. "He made up the word syzygy just to get rid of his letters."

"It's a perfectly good word," Sam declared. "I ran into one of those bright lads who sprung it on me."

Having convinced Williams that he was a prince among men, Sam nimbly invented a fire from a short circuit in a first-floor apartment on Tuesday night.

"That's where the Graces live," Mrs. Williams said. "They've gone out to California to see their daughter. I don't know a thing about a fire. Joe and I were here all evening playing bridge with the Tennelsons. Must have played until nearly one."

"And believe me, if there had been a fire," Williams laughed, "my wife would have known it. She's ready to put in a call if she smells a cigarette smoldering in an ashtray. At me all the time."

Sam studied them shrewdly. Then he thanked them and took his departure. The Williamses were telling the truth, he was ready to bank on that. Paul Brooks had an alibi that would hold.

III

Three pairs of eyes followed Mr. Potter as he crossed the library to the telephone. An earlier call had been answered so cryptically that the Brennings could make nothing of it except that he had talked to a man named Sam. This time he said cheerfully, "Oh, yes, Opal. How did you make out?"

He listened for a long time. "Well," he said at length. "No one there. She was positive? I mean, the kind of person whose opinion you could rely on? . . . Well, then, that seems to be that . . . Not really surprised . . . No, nothing else. Thanks more than I can say . . . Yes, I heard from him."

He came back slowly, deep in thought. "Joan," he said, "how about a game of billiards?"

She got up in relief. "Anything for a change," she agreed.

When they had gone into the billiard room he closed the door behind him. She giggled nervously.

"Why, Hiram!"

"When we were driving back from New York," he reminded her, "I told you there was going to be a lot of checking up. It's your turn now. Who is Mr. Owen of Baltimore?"

"I won't tell you."

He leaned against the door, hands in his pockets, with the air of a man prepared for a long siege.

"You'll have to tell me, you know."

"You can't make me."

"I won't have to. You're going to be eager to tell me."

She laughed. "Why?"

"Because one of four men killed Ann Kenyon on Tuesday night. That was obvious from the beginning. That means alibis. Only one of those four men has an alibi that will stand up and that is Paul Brooks. So we're left with Charlie, Glen and Jerome. One of them is a killer, Joan. A cold-blooded killer of women."

"You're trying to trick me," she said contemptuously. "I happen to know Jerome Cook went to see that neurotic sister of his. Emily mentioned it."

Mr. Potter shook his head. "I just had a little checking job done. Friend of mine called on Cook's sister, Mrs. Fitch, in Stamford. Jerome wasn't there on Tuesday. Mrs. Fitch was alone. The neighbor next door had just moved in and didn't have a telephone. She used Mrs. Fitch's to call a doctor and looked around to see how the furniture had been placed. There wasn't a soul in the place but Mrs. Fitch herself."

Joan watched Mr. Potter. Her look of confidence turned to uncertainty. She bit her lips. At length she yielded. "All right," she said, "you win. I can give Jerome Cook an alibi. I spent the night with him. He is Mr. Owen of Baltimore. I don't expect you to understand; I know he doesn't seem a bit glamorous, but he's simply wonderful. I'm sorry for Emily but she's too old to compete—in a way."

"He used his sister as a cover, didn't he?"

"Well, he's very fond of Emily, after all. He didn't want to hurt her. Neither," Joan added virtuously, "do I."

"Do you expect to marry him?"

"I suppose not," Joan admitted. "It doesn't even matter. If you tell my parents they'll about go crazy. I don't expect anyone to understand how it is. Perhaps I'm just no good and I couldn't care less. I can't figure it myself. But I'm crazy about him. If I have to go on the witness stand to protect him, I'll do it, even if it blasts my reputation sky high. Because he is in the clear. He was with me."

"And why Mr. Owen?"

"Well, he had this car with Maryland plates under that name."

"Why?"

She shifted her feet, turned away to avoid his eyes. "He did a job down there as an architect a long time ago. I guess maybe he had a girl there and didn't want to get caught. I've got sense enough to know I'm not the only one. Women will always fall for Jerome. He knows all there is to know about them." She made a helpless gesture. "It's no use. I can't explain."

"It isn't necessary," he said dryly. "So he just kept renewing the driving license as Mr. Owen and went down to Maryland when he was supposed to visit his sister. Quite a busy little man. You were talking to him on the telephone when I first got here, weren't you?"

She nodded. A dull red flush crept over her face. "I know. The girl without pride, chasing a man, begging him—sometimes I don't know what's got into me."

"He didn't want any part of it?"

"Not at first," she admitted.

"But you made your plans that night at dinner?"

She nodded again.

He still lounged against the door. "So that's why you insisted on Brooks coming to dinner and flirted with Charlie Forbes. A little smoke screen."

She nodded again, a shamed look in her eyes for all the defiance of her mouth. "I had to," she muttered. "I had to. I wouldn't have dared make any scandal because he—really likes Emily. I don't think he'd ever leave her. He doesn't even pretend about that. But I'm mad about him. And you needn't look so concerned. At least it's human to be in love and it's not human to kill. You're left with Glen or Charlie. I don't know which it was and frankly I don't much care."

19

"Just a tiny piece of white meat," Emily insisted.

Jerome leaned back in his chair and laughed. "You've already forced Blair and Glen to eat more than they want. Emily, my sweet, you can't cure the effects of mob malice by another helping of turkey."

Emily smiled reluctantly. "I don't know what I'm thinking of. But I was so upset. Throwing rocks and breaking windows—it's so ugly."

"Ugly, yes," Jerome agreed, "but petty. It sounds to me like a group of irresponsible teen-agers."

"Stanley Brenning thinks Paul Brooks is behind it," Emily said.

"When did you see Stan?" Forbes asked his sister sharply.

"He came by this afternoon. He was so worried about your new will." Emily broke off in embarrassment. "I told him it was your own business."

"So it is," Forbes agreed. "Look, Emily, would you mind if we skip dessert? After that meal I couldn't eat another bite. Anyhow, I'd like to talk to Blair." He turned to her. "Will you go for a walk or are you too tired?"

"Glen," Emily protested, "it's pouring. You can't drag that girl out in the rain."

"Sorry, I hadn't noticed. It was clear when I got here."

"We could take the station wagon," Blair suggested.

There was a curious stillness and then Forbes said, "Yes, we could do that. Do you mind doing the driving at night?"

"Not at all."

Blair had been driving for a quarter of an hour with no sound but the rain drumming on the roof, the rhythmical movement of the windshield wipers, the occasional splash as the car went through a puddle. Beside her, Glen had not spoken. She waited, wondering what his new mood would be. He had been so many things in a day, terrifying in his anger, passionate in his love making, strange in his very silence while Mr. Potter had talked, and rough in the impatience with which he had told her that everything had changed.

When he did speak it was without preliminaries, abruptly. "I love you. It's curious. Aside from a couple of schoolboy infatuations I've never even thought I was in love. There have been women but they didn't matter. And," he added deliberately, "my two wives, of course. I think it is high time I talked to you about my two wives, Blair. After this morning, when the situation got out of hand, I'd like to have you understand about my marriages.

"I'd known Connie for years, grew up with her. She was good looking, breezy, a lot of fun, companionable as long as she was swimming or playing tennis or dancing or generally being active in some such way. I was fond of her. We more or less drifted into marriage. Almost from the beginning I knew it wouldn't work out. We didn't have enough in common, not enough that mattered. And then she—was killed."

A match flared as he lighted a cigarette. Blair kept her eyes on the black surface of the road, shining under the rain. The windshield wipers moved back and forth, ticking like a heart beat.

"A couple of years later I got the idea of the Center and began to work on it. I was sending out a lot of letters of inquiry to people who might have useful ideas and I needed a secretary to write the letters and handle the details. The girl I hired was Evelyn Harrison. She was young, a shy kid who had been neglected, a pathetic little waif. I don't think anyone had ever bothered to be kind to her. Under a little simple human kindness she blossomed. She was heart-breakingly grateful."

He was silent again for a long time. "Well," he went on heavily, "we were together a lot, working and talking and planning. She was enthusiastic about the Center. And she fell in love with me. We were both lonely and there was something very warming about her devotion, something very flattering about her admiration. The upshot was that I married her.

"She was sweet. Very sweet. And I had a great deal of affection for her. In some ways, I came closer to finding real contentment with Evelyn than I ever knew with Connie. And yet no one understood that marriage. The people who liked me thought I was a fool. The people who didn't like me thought the Harrisons had some hold on me, that I'd been blackmailed into marriage. Queer, isn't it?"

Blair swerved to avoid a deer, which had wandered onto the highway, and righted the car again.

"Well, that's the story of my marriages. Then I met you and fell in love with you. And I don't know what to do about it. I can't ask you to marry me. Twice married and half the town, at this point, believes I killed both girls and Miss Kenyon as well. As," he went on stiffly, "I really did kill a man once, long ago. So I want you to go away, Blair. Go away at once, please. Every man has his breaking point and I want you to go before I reach mine."

Blair slowed, made a U turn, dimmed the lights as a car approached them and then stopped with a soft cry, putting one hand over her eyes.

"What is it?" Forbes asked quickly.

"Sorry," she said. "Every now and then it happens when I drive at night. Oncoming lights blind me and my pupils just don't adjust as they should. I'll be all right after a while."

The door on his side of the car opened and closed and he came around to her side. "Move over," he said. "I may be neurotic about driving but I don't expect you to do it under the circumstances."

Without a word Blair moved over to the far side of the seat and Forbes climbed in. For a moment he sat with his hands gripping the wheel. He took out a handkerchief, mopped his head, wiped the palms of his hands. Then with a sharply indrawn breath he released the brake.

He drove almost at a crawl, face tense, eyes staring, knuckles white as he clung to the wheel.

"I wonder," Blair said at length, "if it has occurred to you that you haven't given me much choice."

"What do you mean?"

"You haven't asked me whether I'd like to stay."

His head swung around to her. "Blair!"

"Glen!" she screamed. "Careful!" She pulled hard on the wheel and the car skidded viciously on the wet road but it missed the passing car it had so nearly sideswiped. "I thought you could drive."

"I thought you had night blindness," he said pleasantly. "It seems that we were both mistaken."

II

The spring shower had stopped by the time they reached the Cook house, and the shredded clouds floated across the moon. Blair went into the house quickly, after a good night which Glen answered coolly. She ran up the stairs, relieved that neither Emily nor Jerome was in the living room. She did not want to talk to them. She did not want to talk to anyone.

What had possessed her to trick Glen into driving the car? Some preposterous idea that she could help restore his confidence. Some dim hope that if he could believe in himself he would let her stay. Because she had fallen in love with him and unless she could break down the barrier between them it would be no use. And instead she had nearly killed them both and Glen had lost his nerve. She had made everything worse. Whatever slim chance they might have had of salvaging happiness out of the wreckage was gone now and she had destroyed it herself.

The telephone rang and rang. Blair waited for one of the Cooks to answer it but they must be sleeping soundly. At length the persistent ringing got on her nerves and she ran down the stairs.

"Blair?"

"Yes." Her heart thumped. The voice was a husky whisper.

"This is Charlie. The damnedest thing has happened. I've found out why Miss Kenyon was killed and who did it."

"What!"

"Yes. I tried to reach Potter but he's out somewhere."

"Speak louder. I can barely hear you."

"I can't. Someone is listening. Look, I'm in a jam. He's leaving now. If we're going to clear Glen we've got to hurry. Can you meet me?"

"Where?"

"Miss Kenyon's bungalow. That's where he's heading. I'll follow. Oops. I've got to hurry. Don't waste any time."

Blair ran back for her coat and then went down to the station wagon. The ignition key was gone. Glen must absently have pocketed it. She hesitated and then, reaching in the glove compartment for a flashlight, set off on foot, the light bobbing after her.

It was not until she reached the entrance to the covered bridge that she stopped short. This was where it had happened, where two women had been trapped on foot. She had come like a fool, a gullible fool.

Make up your mind, she told herself. You've got to make up your mind. Do you trust the Forbes men or don't you? Suppose it's true—suppose Charlie has found something that will clear Glen, that will make everything right for us.

The minutes were ticking away and Charlie was waiting. Anyhow, she reminded herself, it only happened to Glen's wives, only to the women to whom he'd left his money.

She thrust her hand in her pocket, pulled out Mr. Potter's police whistle and started through the bridge, gripping it so hard it hurt her hand. She had covered nearly three-quarters of the distance when she heard the clatter of the loose floor boards. She looked back but could not see the exit. Something blocked it. At the same moment, the headlights came on, blinding her, and the motor roared.

She put the whistle to her lips and blew. Then she whirled and ran at top speed, coat flying, feet pounding. *He's going to kill me. He's going to kill me. Kill me.*

A horn sounded insistently, echoing through the bridge. Brakes screamed.

Blair was at the opening now and she hurled herself to the left, away from the road, skidded down the bank, clutching at bushes, while the flashlight and whistle rolled down into the river below. She heard two cars clatter through the bridge. The first went on, gathering speed. The second stopped and a man shouted, "Blair! Blair! Where are you? Are you hurt? Blair, it's Potter. It's all right. You're safe."

She called out and in a few moments saw a flashlight bobbing overhead. Then there was a scrambling sound as Mr. Potter let himself down the bank. He stretched out his hand, seized hers and, with unexpected strength, pulled her up slowly until she could get to her feet. She clung to him, sobbing. Over them the bridge vibrated as a car went through. When it was quiet again she said, "He was going to kill me. You saved my life by blowing the horn to scare him, show him he was followed, his car seen."

"I owed you that. How did he trap you in that bridge on foot?"

Blair told him about Charlie's telephone call and that she couldn't use the station wagon because the key was missing.

"Mr. Potter, how did you happen to be there?" she

asked when he had helped her into the convertible.

"I've been keeping an eye on you," he said grimly. "I was behind all the time."

"You—know the car?"

"Oh, yes."

"Where has he gone?"

"I think he came back while we were under the bridge."

"Wasn't that dangerous?"

"Anything he does now is dangerous. But it was safer to come back. He has to be here."

Mr. Potter turned in on the gravel driveway. The station wagon was where Glen had left it but the key had been returned. Blair stared at it in disbelief. She was too numb for pain but she knew that would come later.

"Blair!" Mr. Potter called. "Come here."

She walked around the station wagon, saw the crumpled figure of the man lying on the gravel beside it.

"Who is he?" Mr. Potter demanded.

"George Harrison, the bookkeeper. Is he dead?"

"He's dead. No," he added sharply, "you can't faint now. I need your help. We can't leave him here. Help me lift him into the station wagon. That's right."

When they had put him down in the back Mr. Potter helped her into the front seat.

"Where are you going?" she asked at last, dully.

"To the hospital. Someone tried to strangle him, but he's still alive. I was just figuring that perhaps he had better stay dead for a while. Someone might have been watching."

Blair made no answer. She sat quietly beside him until they reached the hospital and attendants came with a stretcher to carry Harrison inside.

"I'm going in," Mr. Potter told her. "I've got to talk to Harrison as soon as he is conscious."

"I'll wait here."

"You were never more mistaken in your life," Mr. Potter told her. "You are coming with me. I'm not going to let you out of my sight until that cold-blooded killer is locked up tighter than a drum."

Numbly, Blair let him help her out of the station wagon, lead her into a lobby whose bright lights made her blink. After a few moments an intern, looking very young and scrubbed in a white jacket, brought her a steaming cup of coffee, and sat beside her while she drank it with the air of a man who is not to be moved.

She realized dimly that Mr. Potter had staked out a guard to protect her but she did not feel safe. She felt nothing at all. She was empty, drained of all emotion. And that was the best time. For after the stimulating coffee had its effect she began to suffer.

The young intern watched her anxiously, talking a blue streak without awaiting any reply. Blair did not hear him. He tried to kill me. He tried to kill me.

Upstairs in a private room Mr. Potter sat beside the bed looking down at George Harrison.

"You'd better wait until morning to talk to him," the doctor said, controlling his curiosity.

"I can't wait. Someone nearly murdered him tonight. I've got to talk to him now—before there is any more killing."

At length Harrison stirred, reached up a groping hand to investigate his painful throat, opened his eyes. He looked at Mr. Potter with surprised eyes, at the hospital room with puzzled eyes, remembered and stared around him with frantic eyes.

"I am Hiram Potter," said the man seated beside his bed. "I found you and brought you to the hospital. Now I expect you to talk and talk fast."

Harrison had recuperated quickly from his terror. The small eyes in the big face blinked as he thought fast.

"Let's not misunderstand each other," Mr. Potter said. "There's no money in this for you. You see, I know who tried to kill you tonight and I know why. But there are a few details I'd like cleared up. Before you get in so deep that you can't get out, you had better do some fast talking."

George moaned, clutched at his throat, croaked hoarsely. The doctor, watching this closely, took his wrist.

"Can he talk?" Mr. Potter asked.

The doctor laughed and put down the hand. "He can talk."

20

The intern was still chatting breezily when Mr. Potter came back. He touched Blair's shoulder and was shocked by her white face, the pain in her eyes when she turned to him.

"We're going now," he said gently. "There won't be much more. Think you can take it?"

She nodded, got to her feet and accompanied him lethargically to the station wagon. She could go on and on like this and it wouldn't matter. Nothing would matter again. She displayed no curiosity when Mr. Potter, who seemed to have no particular destination in mind, drove from bar to bar, stopping to look in, going on again. It was close to midnight when he found Charlie Forbes.

"A hell of a time for a conference," Charlie grumbled. "What has happened now?"

"Come along. I don't want to have to tell this more than once."

"Then something has happened. Blair—is Blair all right?"

"Why shouldn't she be?"

Charlie left the bar without protest and followed him out to the car. He gave a little exclamation of surprise when he saw Blair in the front seat. It seemed to him that she shrank as he spoke to her so he climbed in back and sat in grim silence.

There was a light in the salt box at the Center and Forbes, fully dressed, came down to open the door. He stood looking at Blair in stunned surprise and then turned to the two men.

"What's happened?" he asked sharply.

Charlie shrugged. "I don't know. This is Potter's idea of fun and games."

Forbes led them up to his sitting room, lighted a fire and mixed highballs.

"Well," he said at last, "what is it all about?"

"The killer," Mr. Potter said quietly. "He went on the prowl again tonight. He very nearly got Blair and he did get George Harrison."

"Good God!" Charlie exclaimed.

Forbes looked searchingly at Blair, seeking for signs of injury. Only when he was sure that she was all right did he turn to meet Mr. Potter's steady eyes.

"Then you know who he is."

"Oh, yes," Mr. Potter said. "I've been pretty sure since yesterday, and there never was much doubt, you know."

Forbes set down his drink with a shaking hand. "I suppose not. And now Harrison is dead."

"I didn't intend to mislead you. Harrison wasn't killed. He was nearly strangled but his attacker was pressed for time. He had to get the station wagon back to the house before I could follow him. He found Harrison there, snooping around. I got back before he could finish the job. Harrison is in the hospital, under guard, but he talked. He is the one who caused the sabotage here today, put the kids up to throwing rocks and singing 'Sister Ann'; he called off the workmen. Trying to force you to take him back. But he got too curious."

Neither Forbes nor Charlie moved.

"This afternoon I gave you the main outlines of the situation. The killer had to be one of four men. Paul Brooks has an alibi that will hold up. He spent the night with his mistress. He always did on Tuesdays, a fact that was probably known to half the town. I had a little talk with him this afternoon. He had jumped at a chance to use the gossip against you because he wanted to get hold of the land. How much of it he really believed, God knows.

"Anyhow, he was out of the picture and that left three of you. Jerome Cook was supposed to be with his sick sister, a set-up planned to keep Emily from knowing about his—ah—extra-curricular activities. But when his alibi blew up—a neighbor found his sister alone that night—Joan Brenning admitted that she had spent Tuesday night in a New York motel with him."

"Joan! I don't believe it," Forbes declared.

Charlie said limply, "Well, I'm damned."

"Which left," Mr. Potter said, "you two, neither of you with an alibi, or rather both of you with an incredibly tall story."

"I told you the whole business was rigged to get me out of the way, without the prayer of an alibi," Charlie said.

Forbes shook his head. "No, Charlie. Not any more. I should have seen it months ago but I didn't want to. I guess I've been so used to covering up for you that it has become a habit."

Charlie stared at him, face empty.

"I kept hearing about you and Connie," Forbes went on, "but I thought I knew you both, that you just took her out when she wanted to go somewhere and that was all there was to it."

"So help me God, Glen," Charlie said, "that's all there ever was to it."

"But when it comes to Evelyn," Forbes continued as though his cousin had not spoken, "something was mighty wrong."

"God, I never saw her alone in my life. Oh, yes, one night when you were away she called me, thought there was a prowler. I went over the grounds, locked up the house for her and left."

Forbes sat brooding. He might have been deaf. "I didn't believe it about the girls because I couldn't endure to believe it. But when you brought Kenyon here to point a finger at me—"

"Stop, Glen, stop!" Charlie implored him. "Good God, I'd have covered for you whatever you did. I thought you were a combination of schoolboy hero and

big brother and God Almighty. I wouldn't have believed you could sink to this."

He dropped his head on his folded arms and cried.

II

He's telling the truth, Blair thought. He's telling the
truth. Glen, can't you see that? And looked at Glen
and knew that he saw it, too. The years seemed to drop
away; he looked younger.

"Charlie!" He stood beside his cousin, one hand on
the heaving shoulder. "Charlie!" He seemed unable to
find other words but in any case they would have been
unnecessary.

Charlie raised his head, brushed the back of his
hand across his eyes and looked up. For a moment the
Forbes men regarded each other steadily.

Then Glen said, "I won't apologize because I don't
know how. I don't even understand it. The thing just
built up. The rumors about Connie and you, and then
all those accidents with your car. I got to wondering
whether you had killed them accidentally and, when
things got worse, whether you had done it deliberately.
That's why I finally went to Potter. If I was right I
didn't want to be the one—but the thing had to stop.
And then—Blair came."

"Yes," Charlie said sadly, "Blair came."

"I was struck all of a heap. The long-awaited guest.
All that. And that first day you got interested in her,
too, offered to take her home. So I blew my top. And
that night at the Brennings you nearly ran her down."

Charlie ran a shaking hand over his face. "I can't
explain it," he muttered. "Three or four times in my
life I've blacked out from sheer rage." He smiled
crookedly. "The much-publicized Forbes temper. It
was a kind of accumulation that night: you turning on
me in front of Blair, Brooks being impossible, Miss
Kenyon coming out with that hysterical outburst, the
killer who had to be smoked out. I was so mad that,
literally, I couldn't see. Every time I think of it, I get

the horrors. I am going to join you among the ranks of the nondrivers."

Tentatively, almost shyly, Charlie held out his hand and Glen clasped it.

Mr. Potter smiled with unexpected sweetness. "I figured that you two needed some shock treatment to bring you to your senses."

"Some day," Glen told him, but without rancor, "someone is going to break your neck." He dropped his hand on Charlie's shoulder.

"Hey," Blair exclaimed, "what's going on here? Now everyone seems to be in the clear."

"No," Mr. Potter said, "there is still a killer at large."

"But if it isn't Charlie," Forbes demanded, "who is it?"

Mr. Potter looked at him in surprise. "Why, Jerome Cook, of course."

III

Mr. Potter and Charlie were in the front seat of the station wagon and Glen had got in back when Blair ran out of the salt box.

"I'm going with you."

"I don't want you to come," Mr. Potter said. "Jerome has gambled too much to yield quietly. There may be trouble."

She opened the door. "Please let me go with you. Emily is going to need someone. She loves him so much."

She climbed in quickly beside Forbes and Mr. Potter started the motor.

"I simply don't believe it," Forbes said. "Not Jerome of all people."

"This afternoon," Mr. Potter said, "I tried to make you see that he had the only real motive. He wanted your money. That's why he killed Connie and Evelyn. Then, when you decided to support the Center, he lured Miss Kenyon into coming here so no one could miss the Bluebeard angle, the community would reject your gift and send you to the chair."

"Is this more of what Stan calls your supposing?" Forbes asked.

"No, I put your detective, Kurt Tyson, onto it. He has dug up quite a lot. Miss Kenyon's publishers produced a letter asking for her address and it's in Jerome's writing. We checked it with some stuff in Brenning's office."

"But, damn it, man," Charlie said, "you told us yourself that he spent the night with Joan."

"That's what Joan said," Mr. Potter pointed out.

"It seems to me," Charlie said dryly, "that she ought to know."

"Joan was his alibi," Mr. Potter explained. "As Mr. Owen of Baltimore he seems to have had a fairly strenuous love life, out of bounds. I don't think he was interested in Joan. Certainly he didn't want to be tangled with any woman in Bridgetown. If Emily discovered that he was unfaithful, the chances were that all his efforts to get his hands on the Forbes money would be gone. He had evidently discouraged the kid as well as he could.

"But at the Brennings' dinner he met Miss Kenyon, found out that she was a drunk, and in some way betrayed himself to her. So he had to get rid of her fast. But this time he didn't dare rely on his sister. She would cover infidelities but she would never condone murder. So he took a chance on having to explain his infidelity to Emily, agreed to meet Joan in New York, gave her a drink with sleeping pills in it, left her about midnight and came back here, took care of Miss Kenyon and got back some time early in the morning. I knew Joan had been doped the moment I saw her."

"And where did he get all those sleeping pills?"

"Kurt Tyson talked to his sister's physician. He had given her a prescription for sleeping pills some time ago which she claimed to have lost. He refused to refill within so short a space of time. I think we can credit Jerome with opportunity, if nothing else."

"But actually you are just guessing that he left Joan at all."

"Well, not entirely. He made a small slip, one that he almost got by with. The man I had following Joan, fellow named Sam Trumble, just remembered it. When he took his car into the motel that night he parked it with the nose in. When he left in the morning, it had been backed in."

"But why," Forbes said at last, "did he try to kill Blair?"

"Because you, like a damned fool, had just made her your heir." Mr. Potter ignored Blair's gasp of surprise. "Anyhow, with public feeling now stirred to its peak, he wanted to end the situation, get you permanently out of the way. He saw you two return in the station wagon tonight, saw Forbes walk off, leaving the key in the ignition, pocketed it and telephoned Blair from the drugstore. Then when Blair had to walk, he followed in the station wagon. Unfortunately for him, I was waiting and followed him. When I blew my horn, he didn't dare kill her."

"Can you prove any of this?" Charlie asked.

"You forget that Harrison was snooping, saw Jerome return in the station wagon. Jerome tried to strangle him. We have Harrison's testimony. We also have one fingerprint on a drinking glass containing barbiturates that was on Miss Kenyon's table. We haven't been able to check it yet, of course, but I'm willing to bet on it being Cook's. The glass had been wiped but he was in a hurry and careless. A killer is bound to be a vain man, too sure of himself to be careful because he has contempt for the intelligence of other people.

"So, Harrison's testimony, plus the missing sleeping pills, plus the letter of inquiry about Miss Kenyon sent to her publisher, plus the car which was moved from the motel in the night, plus—above all—the motive—and I think we've got all we need."

"Poor Emily," Forbes said. "Poor girl." He reached for Blair's hand and held it tightly.

Mr. Potter rang the bell and after a pause rang

again. In a few minutes Jerome, in pajamas and slippers, tying the belt of his robe around him, opened the
door. He blinked in surprise when he saw Mr. Potter
with Blair.

"Good heavens," he exclaimed. "You poor girl! I
thought you had gone to bed hours ago. Sorry you
were locked out."

Mr. Potter followed Blair into the hallway and Charlie and Glen crowded close behind.

Jerome was startled. "What a delegation! Has anything happened?"

"George Harrison was strangled tonight," Mr. Potter
said.

"Harrison!" Jerome was aghast. "Who would
want—" His eyes traveled to Forbes and he looked
anxious. "I hope to God no one hears about that row
you had with him today, Glen."

"How did you hear about it?" Glen asked.

Jerome's eyes flickered. "How does anyone hear
what he does in this town? Let's not talk too loud.
Emily is asleep."

Blair said sharply, "She was here, asleep, all the
time that telephone rang and rang?"

Glen turned with a swift movement and tore up the
stairs. They could hear him pounding on the door,
shouting, "Emily! Emily!"

Jerome knew then, knew by the frantic fear in
Glen's voice, by the faces confronting him. He took a
step backward and remembered that he was dressed in
pajamas and slippers. He could not get away like that.

Upstairs, the heavy pounding stopped. "Yes, it's
Glen. I'm coming in." A door shut and a murmur of
voices went on and on.

If Blair had been in doubt before, she felt no doubt
now. Jerome's eyes moved from face to face with an
expression of puzzled annoyance but he was gray. He
asked no questions. He did not speak at all. Blair
watched him in horror and fascination. The incredible
thing was that there was no change in him at all
beyond his pallor and that uncharacteristic caution that

kept him from speaking. He looked as jovial as ever. No outward sign to betray the man who had killed three times; who, a few hours earlier, had tried to run her down.

At length there were stumbling footsteps and Glen came down, his arm around Emily. She wore a shabby wool robe and her hair was disheveled.

"She's all right," Glen said. "Not more than one sleeping pill apparently."

Emily shook off his arm and went straight to Jerome, put her hands on his shoulders, looked deep in his eyes.

"Glen has gone mad," she said. "He's been telling me—he said you killed all those women: killed Connie and Evelyn and Miss Kenyon; that you nearly killed Blair, that you killed George Harrison tonight."

"No," Mr. Potter said, "he didn't kill Harrison. Harrison is very much alive and highly talkative."

It was the change in Jerome's expression that made Emily drop her hands from his shoulders as though they had been burned. She recoiled. The warmth that had been her great charm was gone. She seemed to Blair to age and shrink, to die little by little before her eyes.

At last she said thickly, "It's true. I can see it in your face. It's true. I wouldn't believe Glen but I see it in your face. I adored you and all the time you were—capable of that. Perhaps you even made love to me after—" her hands gripped together.

"I've guessed for a long time that you weren't faithful but I'd never been pretty, I thought perhaps I expected too much. I knew you were lazy and extravagant. My parents begged me not to marry you. But I couldn't help it. I was mad about you."

She sounded like Joan, Mr. Potter thought.

Jerome took a step toward her. "Emily," he said.

She looked at him in a kind of wonder. "Do you still think you have only to call me? There's nothing left now. Nothing at all." She turned away and stumbled toward the stairs.

Jerome stared after her. A stout man, harmless to look at. He made no attempt to follow Emily. There was no appeal from the finality in her voice. He stood waiting like an actor who has forgotten his lines, looking foolish and pathetic in his pajamas and slippers, bald head gleaming under the light.

Unbelievably, he summoned up a smile and a chuckle. "This is ridiculous, of course. Perfectly ridiculous. But it will be a simple matter to straighten out. I think I'll put in a call for my lawyer."

"That last gamble," Mr. Potter said quietly. "Forbes, you had better get his clothes together. Pack a bag. He won't be coming back."

IV

As the taxi came around the Gramercy Park Hotel Blair noticed that the gardeners were busy removing tulips and replacing them with other flowers. In the short time of her absence the season had already advanced and changed. She got out in front of Mr. Potter's house and went up the steps. A big Italian in a fresh white coat admitted her.

Mr. Potter came out of the drawing room and after one searching glance at her made her comfortable in a deep chair, rolled a table beside her, and poured her a glass of sherry.

"We won't talk about decorating the house yet," he said. "Have you had any sleep?"

"Not a great deal," she admitted. "Dr. Evans offered me some sleeping pills but—" she shivered. She took the cigarette he offered her and leaned forward for a light. Her eyes fell on the book lying on the table: *The Frightened Women* by Ann Kenyon.

"Sorry," Mr. Potter said. "I forgot about that." He picked the book up, turned it over in his hand. "Sometimes I wonder how much that poor woman's morbid imagination did in setting the atmosphere for her own murder. The whole place was permeated with the Bluebeard idea. If it hadn't been that the motive was so overwhelmingly obvious or that Harrison had been too curious, Jerome might have got away with it."

"Or if you hadn't been there," Blair said. She leaned forward. "You wouldn't let Glen thank you but I can't forget you saved my life and you probably saved Glen from a murder charge. What do you think will happen now?"

"The autopsy on Miss Kenyon revealed a fatal dose of barbiturates, the same kind Mrs. Fitch's doctor had prescribed for her. The Grand Jury has indicted Cook for murder. Nothing can be done about the deaths of Connie and Evelyn. However, the fact that we can prove he drove the car that nearly ran you down will achieve the main object, clear Glen of any more suspicion. No, Jerome Cook lost his last gamble."

"Poor Emily," Blair said. "She's really rather magnificent. Glen wanted to send her abroad until—it's all over, but she refused to go. She is helping him at the Center and people are rallying around. They can't do enough for both of them to make up for the way they have behaved."

"And what about you?" Mr. Potter asked.

"Well, I seem to be out of a job. I'm going to get to work on your house, paint the walls, put in some clear colors, replace that heavy furniture with light comfortable pieces—"

"And Forbes?"

Blair smiled ruefully. "What can I do?" she demanded. "What with all the scandal, he is being the soul of chivalry. He won't ask me to marry him and I can't very well propose to him."

"Why not?" Forbes demanded from the doorway, his voice edged with laughter.

Blair turned and saw him coming toward her.

BESTSELLERS
FROM DELL

fiction

- [ ] ERIC by Doris Lund.............................. $1.75 (4586-04)
- [ ] MARATHON MAN by William Goldman.......... $1.95 (5502-02)
- [ ] WINTER KILLS by Richard Coneon.............. $1.75 (6007-00)
- [ ] THE OTHER SIDE OF MIDNIGHT by Sidney Sheldon $1.75 (6067-07)
- [ ] THE RHINEMANN EXCHANGE by Robert Ludlum.. $1.95 (5079-13)
- [ ] THE LONG DARK NIGHT by Joseph Hayes....... $1.95 (4824-06)
- [ ] SHAMPOO by Robert Alley..................... $1.75 (7808-17)
- [ ] PLEASURE MAN by Mae West................... $1.50 (7074-06)
- [ ] THE NAKED FACE by Sidney Sheldon............ $1.25 (4921-05)
- [ ] DOG DAY AFTERNOON by Patrick Mann......... $1.50 (4519-06)
- [ ] THE BOY WHO INVENTED THE BUBBLE GUN
      by Paul Gallico $1.50 (0719-28)

nonfiction

- [ ] JAMES DEAN, THE MUTANT KING by David Dalton $1.75 (4893-02)
- [ ] MIKE ROY'S CROCK COOKERY................. $1.25 (5617-04)
- [ ] THE FEMALE WOMAN by Anianna Stassinopoulous. $1.50 (5015-02)
- [ ] MAN KIND? by Cleveland Amory............... $1.75 (5451-03)
- [ ] CHARLES BRONSON SUPERSTAR by Steven Whitney $1.50 (4561-11)
- [ ] THE JAWS LOG by Carl Gottlieb............... $1.50 (4689-00)
- [ ] THE REICH MARSHAL by Leonard Mosley........ $1.75 (7686-06)
- [ ] JOEY by Donald Goddard..................... $1.75 (4825-05)
- [ ] DR. STILLMAN'S 14-DAY SHAPE-UP PROGRAM
      by I. M. Stillman, M.D., and S. S. Baker.......... $1.75 (1913-04)
- [ ] WHY MEN CALL GIRLS by Shannon Canfield
      and Dick Stuart $1.50 (9609-06)

Buy them at your local bookstore or send this page to the address below:

DELL BOOKS
P.O. BOX 1000, PINEBROOK, N.J. 07058

Please send me the books I have checked above. I am enclosing $_____
(please add 25¢ per copy to cover postage and handling). Send check or
money order—no cash or C.O.D.'s.

Mr/Mrs/Miss_____

Address_____

City_____State/Zip_____

This offer expires 11/76